HERITAGE HISTORY

History with an American Family Saga

First Edition

i

Heritage History

Vallie Jo Whitfield

WHITFIELD BOOKS

LIBRARY OF CONGRESS
Catalog Card Number 87-050111

FIRST EDITION
Published August 1987

International Standard Book Number
0-930920-17-1 Hard bound

Typography
BURNS TYPESETTING SERVICE
Concord, California

PRINTED IN THE UNITED STATES

WHITFIELD BOOKS
1841 Pleasant Hill Road
Pleasant Hill, California 94523

FOREWORD

A sincere purpose to preserve facts and personal memoirs that are deserving of preservation, and which unite the present to the past is the motive for the American family saga and history.

From Germany they came in the 1820s and 1830s to America and crossed part of a continent to make a home in Indiana along the Ohio River. They endured the Civil War and tragedies. The women carried on contributing notably to the communities. A family of candymakers helped to start the industry. From these men a new generation arose during a time of world wars and industrial progress. Families were born again and the happenings of the country made reliable changes in the United States.

To identify origins and time and be authentic the original source and documents are used in the book to make it a reliable, factual account of American history.

TABLE OF CONTENTS

ILLUSTRATIONS

ILLUSTRATIONS

PHOTOGRAPHS

PHOTOGRAPHS

Chapter One

The word Heiner is a family name. The root word for Heiner was found in Saxony near Heinersdorf. In the study of the name there was found the names of Hoen, Huner, Hoener, Heener. Heiner had changed to Hiner. These families were of the Protestant Faith, as a result of the Reformation, and were residents in the predominantly Catholic Duchy of Julich.

The German name Heiner, Hyner, Hayner, Humer possibly derived from the word *"Haginer"* which means *"master of a hedged-in dwelling"* which indicated a farmer or landholder. Another authority on names groups it with names meaning *"strong as a hedge."*

A title might have been given one of the early Heiner ancestors for some outstanding deed, performing, or characteristic, and there is the possibility that the Coat-of-Arms could have been awarded for some such deed. Heiner Arms is found in the *"Wappenbuch"* by Siembacher, and is the only one found, and in the section allotted to Saxony. The golden cock in the lower half of the shield on a green so-called Dreiberg (Three Hills) is exactly the same position as the three branches of the rose in the upper half of the shield.

According to Dr. Alfred Jaeger of Munich, Germany, each of the nations of Germany originally had two colors into which the shield was divided, one the ground color and the other the figure represented upon it. The colors were the same in every family belonging to the same nation, the figures alone varying. Saxons were black and white; French shields were white and red; Bavarians were white and blue; Swabians, red and

1

yellow. Ancient colors of four principal nations of Germany.[1]

These nations of Germany had regional boundaries which changed often with the rapid succession of different reigning families, increased population, disputes and war. The nineteenth century was a time the country had these geographical regions: Brandenburg, Brunswick, Hannover, Holstein, Mecklenburg-Schwerin, Prussia, Saxony, Schleswig, and Westphalia in the northern part of Germany. Alsace, Baden, Bavaria, Hesse, Hesse Nassau, Lorraine, Rhine, Wurttemberg were regions in the southwestern part of Germany. East Prussia, Pomerania, Posen, Silesia, West Prussia were regions in the eastern part of Germany.[2]

In Germany some families lived in economic conditions which impelled each family to make some change, and it was wholly an individual matter. Many of the German citizens chose to move from Europe to the new land of America. A few had a kinship family who had settled in America.

The people made individual journeys down the Rhine river to Rotterdam or other ports. Most of the German immigrants were natives of the Palatine, in southwestern Germany, who had fled to America from wars, religious persecution, decaying economy, or for new opportunity.

The first group left the Palatinate in 1708 under their minister. This stage of migration in Germany was from Rotterdam to one of the English ports. Most of the ships called at Cowes, on Isle of Wight.

In 1776 the American Revolutionary War had started and many Hessians from Germany were imported to help fight the war with the British. Colonies of Germans had formed with families. The Federal Census of 1790 discloses 176,407 Germans living in America. But historians maintain that 225,000 to 250,000 Germans lived in the colonies at the time of the Declaration of Independence.

The bulk of migration came from the Palatinate, Wurtemburg, Baden, Alsace, and the German cantons of Switzerland. From the ports of Germany they left the land for America, and landed at the seaports of New York, Philadelphia, Baltimore, and other coastal ports. During this time came the people with family names of Heiner, Ault, Fox, and many others. From the ports of Germany they left the land for America, and landed in a new world. New York and New Jersey, and Pennsylvania were the places that these people stepped on the soil of the United States. Ault families were first located at New Hampshire and later migrated to other settlements and states. Fox families came from England and Germany, and other places in Europe.

Pennsylvania was a favorite distributing point for these Germans. East coast settlements were to any place. They pushed southward through the beautiful Shenandoah Valley into Maryland, Virginia, North Carolina, and New Jersey. The immigrates trails into the western territory were many in number before the land became part of a Colony or State. Indians inhabited the land but the white men and the black slaves moved into the lands.[3]

The Colonies of America developed slowly. Then for eight years the American Revolution took place from 1773 to 1783. Immigrations numbered, during the quarter-century from 1790 to 1815, at less than two hundred and fifty thousand people.

The frontier war of America in 1812 had quieted the Indian menace, and the peace of 1815 had begun a renewal of the westward flow of population.

Around 1815 several shiploads of Swiss and Wurttembergers disembarked at Philadelphia. The traditional German port; others arrived at New York port, Baltimore port, and other ports. A flow of migration of people from Europe began in the 1830's and continued until 1860, reaching its crest in the years 1847-1854.[4]

Once the people reached a port in the United States they were checked in by the immigration authorities. An oath of allegiance was taken to the country and often this occurred on the boat with groups of men repeating the oath for themselves and their families. There was no formal declaration of their citizenship and few men had naturalization and oaths in a court of their settlement.

The America Colony had been settled. Large land grants existed making the property only available as rentals in areas where people were living. This means of using property accommodated the flow of German immigrants. The territory was spacious with few people. The immigrants had to adjust to new ways in a strange country. The Heiner and Hiner families settled in Warren and Hunterdon Counties of New Jersey state. Others with the names settled in several counties of Pennsylvania, and in Maryland. The rugged Allegheny mountain range tended to separate the two sections of Virginia which made traveling rather difficult. Virginia was so large that after the Civil War the northern portion was split off as West Virginia. A man named John Symmes of New Jersey acquired title to Hamilton County and sections of Warren and Butler Counties, and encouraged settlers from New Jersey to settle in Ohio in the 1790's. Ohio was to experience a flow of people from the east.

The Old Trading Path of Pennslyvania[5]

In the middle of the eighteenth century white men began to cross the Allegheny Mountains and enter the Ohio River Basin. According to the Indians, the route

4

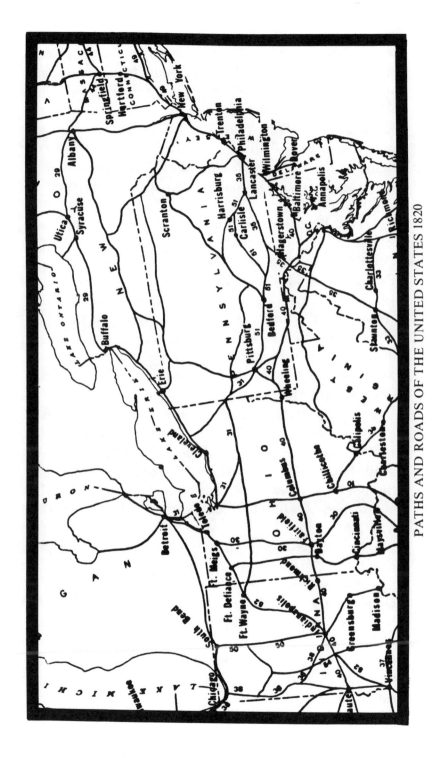

PATHS AND ROADS OF THE UNITED STATES 1820

which ran almost west from Philadelphia to the present site of Pittsburgh was the easiest route from the Atlantic slope through the dense laurel wilderness to the Ohio River. It was an early trail used by white men after the Revolutionary War. This road passed through Lancaster, Carlisle, Bedford and Greensburg. This path followed no streams and crossed only one major stream, the Susquehanna. This path for a road could be traveled any month of the year.

The Pennsylvania Council in 1754 reported the length of this Indian path to be 190 miles. In 1735, the Great State Road of Pennsylvania from Carlisle to Pittsburgh was laid out, and in 1819 it was measured at 197 miles. Later when the Heiner and Hiner families crossed on this route to Ohio they were passing on an Indian route that for over two-thirds of its length passed directly across the many ranges of the great Appalachian Mountains. Later the eastern section of this old Indian trading path, in a portion between Philadelphia and Lancaster, sixty-six miles in length, became the first highway with pressed layers of broken stones in the United States. Pioneer families did not have a paved road but followed trails with hardships, faith, and thrilling experiences; the trails were narrow and of a condition suitable for pack horses and wagons to travel on.

People settled in Eastern Pennsylvania and some crossed the various ranges of the Alleghenies into what is now the western part of the United States. When the Ohio River was reached, a great many of the immigrants had boats or rafts built on which they continued their journey. Pittsburgh, which had the Fort, was usually the embarkation point for the destination in the western territory of Ohio and Indiana. Scotch-Irish, German and English origins followed this route.

A person can glean from the past records how the

immigrants left the eastern seaport on arrival for their destination in the territory. Many people seemed to have reached New York, or New Jersey, and Pennsylvania, and from these locations went to their point of destination. Some did not move so easily and lingered in the eastern states, especially if they had kinship, sponsors, or church and missionary help.

Indiana

In 1816, Indiana became the nineteenth United States. Foreign immigration into Indiana before 1860 numbered 28,584 people foreign born in Germany, and 541,079 native born in Indiana. In 1860 there were 740 foreign born people from Prussia, Germany, and 24,310 native born in New York. In 1860, Jefferson County, Indiana was one of ten counties in that state with the largest number of foreign born which was 3,571 people.

Free Inhabitants in dt. 6 (Market City of Madison) in the County of Jefferson State enumerated by me, on the 11th day of June 1860

Chapter Two

In Germany, a few years later, after the new states were organized under a Constitutional government, the people had America in everybody's mouth. Businessmen talked of it over their accounts. Parents in the family talked of relatives who went to America. Children played at emigrating. People who had relatives in the new land went around reading letters for the enlightenment of less fortunate folks. Many could not read and write but gladly listened to the stories of others.

In Germany, a family talked of their relatives who went to America named Heiner. A young man, John Heiner and his brothers were in America in the 1830's. There they found wives and had families. Many years later a descendant of John Heiner had lost the early history of John Heiner but knew that one generation has someone who tells to its youth the story of the past, and it was so for the Hiners. They told Elizabeth Heiner Fox of Madison, Indiana, and she in turn told stories to her son, Joseph Edward Fox and his wife, Valley Schiefer Fox. The mother, Valley Fox, in turn, told her children. She said that the second period of German migration in America began about 1820 and lasted through the Civil War. *"Your ancestors on your father's side of the family came from Germany. They came by ship from Germany to the Atlantic coast about 1830. Heiner was born in Germany and came with his brothers. They probably came with the family. The family knew people here in the United States and were skilled tradesmen. The Foxes were the best of candy makers, and they made candies called confections and sweet cakes, and sold them for a living. All of Elizabeth and Joseph Fox's sons made candy except your father, Joseph Fox, the son."*

"I knew Elizabeth Fox. She was a Heiner, and a Hiner. She used to tell me all about her family. Her father married a German-born girl in America. She was Elizabeth. They had several children of which most of them were born here. The family travelled by horse and wagon and crossed the Ohio River on flatboats, and they lived along the Ohio River. They settled in Jefferson County about Madison. Many travelers passed through Madison on the north and south road. They moved there when she was a small girl." [1]

The daughter, Vallie Jo Whitfield wrote down the words of her mother. She could not easily locate the Heiner ancestor, and she ceased to try in 1965. She wrote and published the books. **Whitfield History And Genealogy Of Tennessee** in 1964, and **Whitfield McKeel Fox Schiefer Families,** a book published in 1965. The book in 1965 has a short history genealogy on Fox, and it is from the hearsay of her mother. Valley Fox would say that Fox was Fuch in German but this was not correct for no translation ever occurred with the surname. Many years went by. November 1983, Vallie Jo Fox Whitfield was encouraged by the Anna Louck chapter ladies of the National Society Of The Daughters Of The American Revolution to try and gather the documents and papers of her fraternal lineal ancestor. She worked one and a half years studying all of the Heiner and Hiner of Indiana State, and their trails, to learn of her great-grandmother and grandfather. With much work and searching and research she located documents that verified the factual family history.

Heiner and Hiner

In the time of the second period of migration from

Germany to America begins the story. German people were leaving the decaying economy, and seeking new opportunity with kinfolks already in America. They had heard of the new world where there were jobs and freedoms and open doors. It is likely that John Heiner and his brothers came for these reasons. On the entry to the new country it is noted that immigrants of the 1820s and 1830s and later were often torn between giving the accurate answer in a foreign speech accent, or the one they felt would get them in the country. This is the essence of the Heiner-Hiner story, and makes search and research work very difficult. Gaining admittance, or the cause was important. Work was essential to avoid being hungry. Few public records were written. The federal census has been most vital in the search and work on the Heiner-Hiner families.

These people were not very educated. They could barely write the English language. They used the German script of handwriting that they had learned in school. A person studying these records can have difficulty. In some respect it seems best to reprint the records as they exist, even if the records reflect that the people gave information they thought were the right answers to questions, but facts and information were given to help themselves as they saw the situation.

John Heiner Becomes John Hiner

John Heiner was born in 1811 in Soniorse, Germany according to his daughter Elizabeth Hiner.[2] John grew up with his brothers and sisters and went to school in Germany. His parents were Mr. and Mrs. Heiner, and their first names as well as first names of the other members of the family have been misplaced. It is known the Heiner boys left Germany in the 1830's and sailed for the United States. The parents may have

11

accompanied the sons to America.

The Heiner boys, numbering about four young men, were in their twenties. They probably entered the New York port, although Philadelphia, Pennsylvania is often mentioned as the port for German emigrants. The oaths to country were probably made on the boat which crossed the Atlantic Ocean, or at the American port of entry to the United States. They were with the people called INS to America by the immigration authority.

John's stay in Pennsylvania was a few years or a short duration for traveling on the old trading path and crossing the state. In this time the young Heiner men determined what they would like to do. In 1837 John Heiner was in Ohio County, Virginia for he had met the Outh family with a daughter named Elizabeth. On the fourth day of 1837 in the forest of trees and among the spring things they were married making their holy vows in the presence of their brothers and friends, and with consent of her parents.[3] They did not stay in Ohio county very long, and may have been on a westward move in their travels. They were soon crossing the state of Ohio with their traveling companions and coming upon the Ohio River. At the river they boarded a boat, changed at a stop to another boat, and left the boat along the Ohio River at Indiana. Their settlement on land was someplace about Jefferson County on the Indiana side of the river.

In 1840 John and Elizabeth were in Indiana, John's name may be on the census.[4] He was then a head of a family with a wife of age twenty-three, who had a first born child named George, followed by John who was born in 1844. In 1848, the first born daughter Elizabeth was born. She was called Elisa in the family.[5] They were settled in a rental place and tried little farming for John, the father, worked at a trade.

John and Elizabeth made two trips on the Ohio

12

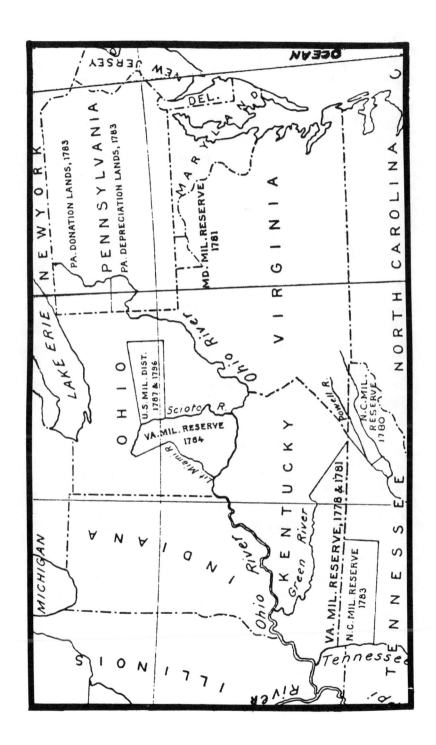

River, and crossed to Kentucky two times in the 1840's. One trip involved checking on two black men named Hiner at Hancock County, Kentucky. They had been set free earlier by traveling white kinship to the territory.[5] The threads for identifying any kinship is very weak with the records of John Heiner.

John Heiner was not a property owner. This meant there were more frequent moves to locate housing. They had two locations in Indiana which was the first place, and later Madison. They never lived in more than three townships in Indiana. In their rental small wooden house in April 1851, Elizabeth gave birth to twin babies, Henry and Atha.

Heiner's name is shortened to Hiner about 1858. John needed more earnings for the growing family, and he found it later at Madison town. James Donnelly opened a shop for making shoes and boots. John Hiner joined the *Boot and Shoe* establishment in the city of Madison. It was located on Broadway bounded by Presbyterian Avenue and Fifth Street. He was a shoe-maker, and appeared in the 1859 Business Directory of Madison, Indiana. John and the family members worked at the shop. George and John, Jr. worked as apprentices at the shoemakers shop.

George Heiner And Camps

The children left school at fifteen years of age. Once they reached a grown-up age they became boarders in their parents' home, and had work to do there. In addition to the work at the shop there was interest in confectionery work. Madison School and the Sabbath School had classes in cooking and the craft of confectionery. It was an education program since 1828. In the 1850's George practiced what he had learned in class.

14

George Heiner was interested in edibles and began food making in quantities at home. On cold winter days the wood fires were keep burning for heating the small house. With their energies and ingenuity they were able to procure chocolates, powdered sugars, and ingredients. These burning fires melted confectioners' sugars, and chocolates. Special recipes known to him alone were a specialty of his home-business. All the children watched the bonbons being made, and the dipping, and swirling of small pieces. His sisters and brothers all helped with the chocolate dipping and coating of the bonbons and frosting. It took many hands and they worked happily together. George taught his brother John to be a confectioner. Their mother worked confecting edible materials. They called it "eatables". George was now twenty-two years of age and still boarding at home.

The decade from 1850 to 1860 was one of growth for the family, as well as the town of Madison, Indiana. There were also changes in the nation at large at this time. It affected people, and was to change the lives of John, Sr., George and John, the junior, and the family. The country was developing but diplomacy became controversial in 1861. The northern and southern parts of the country had different economic conditions with different labor forces. The sectional parts changed with labor economics; and had assumed different value and freedoms. These factors split the country over economics and slavery. It was not a class struggle, but a sectional combat developing that had roots in a complex political, economic, social, and psychological situation for the country.

This controversy on the national level was unfortunate. The south with the Confederates were fighting to keep their independence but the Northerners were fighting for something where independence was for the foreign immigrants also. The union was challenged. In February 1861 six southern states seceded. It was a rousing time for a few places. Madison town called upon its Home Guards. President Abraham Lincoln called on militiamen. Civil War broke out.

Military camps were formed in Indiana. There was an enlistment camp for men at Madison. John Heiner, when age eighteen went to camp, and was mustered in service. George Heiner stayed at home working. One day George with three other men of the town made a plan to take their bakery goods, confections, and foods to sell them to the men at the soldiers' camp.

Along went two small young girls, one of them being George's sister. The men were admitted to the inside of the camp and the food was offered for sale. Soldiers took the confections and ate them. When the sellers asked for payment the men replied that they had no money. George Heiner and a man in camp got into an argument over the eating of the food. Another man witnessing this dispute in the room pulled a gun and shot at George killing him.[6]

There was an investigation and it was unpleasant. Home Guards were needed but soon the whole town was involved in the Civil War, including the Heiner men who gave much in this struggle.

The women had hardships unknown before. Elizabeth Heiner was to face poverty with the children. They all continued to make candies, and work for pay. Four of the family members left home, and Elizabeth was alone with the smaller children.

Chapter Three

~ ~

The state of Indiana's organized military units were 126 Infantry Regiments, 13 Cavalry Regiments, and 26 Batteries of Artillery. For four years Indiana furnished 208,367 sons to the Union cause of the Civil War, including 24,416 who were killed or died during their service with the northern forces.

THREE MAJOR UNDERGROUND
RAILROAD ROUTES IN INDIANA

There were three major routes of the Underground Railroad in Indiana. The Central Route began at the Ohio River crossings and located all the way from Leavenworth to Madison. The railroad helped to move the men and equipment.

There were approximately one hundred military camps, hospitals and other agencies in Indiana during the Civil War. Over seventy of these were regular troop camps. Some of the camps were temporary and of very short duration, 30 to 60 days, and they were closed when the regiments left the state to join the armies in the field.

Each of the eleven congressional districts were authorized camps for rendezvous.

Marion County and Indianapolis, by far, had the majority of the military agencies in the state.

Of the 364,000 on the Union Army side who lost their lives, a third were killed or died of wounds and two-thirds died of disease.[1]

When the Civil War began in 1861, men came together in Indiana. They organized months after the battle began. In August 1862, they located in North Madison at the old State Fairgrounds. In Jefferson County, Indiana there formed Camp Emerson, Camp Jefferson, and Camp Noble. In July 1863, a United States Military Hospital opened in Indiana.

Civil War and John Hiner (1811-1864)

The 137th Regiment Infantry organized by an order of authority on April 23, 1864, with Ed J. Robinson as Commandant, organized rendezvous at Indianapolis. The date for the muster of men into service was May 27, 1864. The period of service was for one hundred days. The date for mustering out was August 1864.

On May 16,1864, John Hiner, age 42, entered at Madison, Indiana, the 137th Regiment, as Private, Company G. At Madison, the command was by Captain McKim. John went to Indianapolis. On May 26, 1864, John Hiner could muster out according to Lieutenant Mills, but he was mustered out of service at Indianapolis on September 21, 1864. Then on October 22, 1864, John Hiner, age 42, born in Germany, entered Recruit Company, 16th Regiment at Indianapolis under Lieutenant Macklin. He was described with dark complexion, blue eyes, black hair and had a height of five

18

| 76 | 137 | Ind. |

John Niner

Put., Capt. McKim's Co., 137 Reg't Indiana Inf.*

Age *42* years.

Appears on

Company Muster-in Roll

of the organization named above.   Roll dated

Indianapolis, Ind., May 26, 1864.

Muster-in to date   *May 26,* 1864.

Joined for duty and enrolled:

When *May 16,* 186 *4.*

Where *Madison*

Period *100* days.

Bounty paid $ 100; due $ 100

Remarks : *Madison Tp., Jefferson Co.*

* This organization subsequently became Co. G, 137 Reg't Ind. Inf.

Book mark :

UNION ARMY. CIVIL WAR.

| 36 | 137 | Ind. |

John Heiner

Pvt., Co. G, 137 Reg't Indiana Infantry.

Appears on

Company Muster Roll

for *May 26 to June 3p 1864.*

Present or absent *Present*

Stoppage $ 1̅0̅0̅ for

Due Gov't $ 1̅0̅0̅ for

Remarks:

Book mark:

UNION ARMY. CIVIL WAR.

feet and five inches. Occupation was shoemaker. This term of service was for one year but before the day was over, John Hiner was mustered out of service by Captain Hager.

In the one hundredth and thirty-seventh Infantry Regiment no one was killed, or died from wounds. Seventeen died of disease, accidents in prison, and other incidents. John Heiner who was enlisted as John Hiner in the Civil War contracted a disease while at camp in Indianapolis. He was sick in November when he returned home to Madison, Indiana. John died on November 4, 1864.

Civil War Pension

Elizabeth Outh Hiner was a widow at age forty-seven with five children. She had no financial support for the family except for what she could earn helping a shoemaker. James Donnelly, the proprietor helped her. She engaged an attorney, John V. Roberts, who filed for a federal pension claim in May 1865.

Elizabeth Hiner did not have clear handwriting. She used extra alphabet symbols in spelling words. It was said she over-wrote words. Although she spoke both German and English, and expressed herself clearly and had good communication.

Elizabeth's pension application and other official papers requiring information were on printed forms of paper filled in by the attorney. The staff members of the pension office, army offices, and court also filled in blank spaces on printed paper forms. These papers have been preserved in the National Archives located in Washington, D.C.

Elizabeth Hiner, and friends as witnesses, furnished information on John Hiner. The government offices

| 76 | 137 | Ind. |

John Hiner

Pvt. , Co. G , 137 Reg't Indiana Infantry.

Appears on

Company Muster Roll

for *July & Aug* , 186*4*.

Present or absent *Present*

Stoppage $ 100 for

Due Gov't $ 100 for

Remarks:

Book mark:

UNION ARMY. CIVIL WAR.

furnished more information from their records which date from 1862 to 1869, and later. Such old records have survived in some cases. The significance of the pension case of Elizabeth Hiner is evident by the authentic records. The underlined words were written in on a typed paper or a form-paper. These records include army cards, letters, and court document.

Civil War Pension

John Hiner (1811-1864) served in the Civil War in two Union Army Regiments in the State of Indiana. Elizabeth Hiner with her attorney requested an army pension in July 1865. The attorney, John V. Roberts filled out an application for the pension. The application was sent to the pension office of the Department of the Interior, and to the Army Adjutant General's office. This application and other papers were filed at the Court in the County of Jefferson, State of Indiana.

The application was filled with this information:

"James Donnelly said, I have been for many years proprietor of Boot And Shoe Establishment at City of Madison in said county. I knew John Hiner and Elizabeth Hiner his wife very intimately. I had two of their sons as apprentices. John Hiner and his wife both frequently worked for me. John Hiner died at Madison United States General Hospital about the 4th day of November 1864. He had a few days before volunteered at Indianapolis, Indiana, procured a furlough started home, took sick, was sent to W.F. General Hospital, died next day, this wife could not ascertain the Company and Regiment to which he belonged. As a friend to the family I went to Indianapolis, and there ascertained that Hiner had volunteered in the 16th Regiment Indiana mounted infantry volunteers but had never

| H_7 | 137 | Ind. |

John Hiner

Put. , Co. G , 137 Reg't Indiana Inf.

Age 42 years.

Appears on **Co. Muster-out Roll,** dated

Indianapolis, Ind, Sept. 21, 1864.

Muster-out to date Sept 21, 1864.

Last paid to Pay due from enlistment, 186 .

Clothing account:

Last settled , 186 ; drawn since $ 100

Due soldier $. 4 45/100 ; due U. S. $ 100

Am't for cloth'g in kind or money adv'd $ 100

Due U. S. for arms, equipments, &c., $ 100

Bounty paid $ 100 ; due $ 100

Remarks: Allowance of Cloth

ing 23.93

Book mark

UNION ARMY. CIVIL WAR.

24

been assigned to any Company of the Regt. I was one of the witnesses to Mrs. Hiner's application for Pension. I know she was the wife of decedent and still his widow. I am not related to her, or interested in her claim or in its prosecuting."

James Donnelly

Attest. W.L. Friedly
Attest. T.J. Humphreys

DECLARATION FOR WIDOW'S ARMY PENSION

State of Indiana
County of Jefferson   ss

On this 23 day of May, A.D., one thousand, eight hundred and sixty-five personally appeared before me David G. Phillips Clerk of the Circuit Court within and for the County and State aforesaid Elizabeth Hiner a resident of Madison in the County of Jefferson and State of Indiana. Age 47 years, who being first duly sworn according to law, doth, on her oath, make the following declaration in order to obtain the benefit of the provisions made by the Act of Congress, approved July 14, 1862. That she is the widow of John Hiner who enlisted in the service of the United States at Indianapolis, in the State of Indiana on the 22 day of October 1864, as a private in Company commanded by   in the 16th Regiment of Indiana Volunteers in the war of 1861; who while in the service aforesaid, and in the line of his duty, died in the United States Hospital at Madison in the State of Indiana on the 4th day of November A.D., 1864. She further declares that she was married to the said John Hiner in the County of Ohio and State of Virginia on the 4 day of April, in the year 1837; that her name before her said marriage was Elizabeth Outh. That her husband, the aforesaid John Hiner, died on the day above mentioned, and that she has remained a widow ever since that period, as will more fully appear by reference to the proof hereto annexed. And further, that the following the names and dates of birth of the only children of the said John Hiner now living, who were under sixteen years of age at the time of his decease, viz: Henry Hiner born on the 20 day of April, 1851, Atha Hiner born on the 20 day of April 1851, Mary Hiner born on the 1 day of May 1854, Margaret Hiner born on the 25 day of November 1857, Ferdinana Hiner born on the 25 day of November 1860, each and all of said children reside in Madison Indiana with applicant. She also declares that she has not, in any manner, been engaged in, or aided or abetted the rebellion in the United States. She hereby appoints John V. Roberts, of Madison States of Indiana, her true and lawful Attorney, with full power of substitution to prosecute this claim for pension, and to receive the certificate which may be issued therefor. She requests that her pension be paid at Madison State of Indiana. Her post office address is Madison County of Jefferson, State of Indiana at time of the death of Hiner he had accompanying furlough-out took sick, on his way home from Indianapolis and was sent to said Hospital where he died the next day.

Signature of Claimant

Elizabeth Hiner

Signature of Witnesses,

James Donnelly
Charles Devon

45?

Hiner　　　*John*

Co. G, **137** Indiana Infantry.
(**100 Days, 1864.**)

Private　　*Private*

CARD NUMBERS.

1	2720345-7	26	
2	2-20355-7	27	
3	2720364-9	28	
4	2720374-0	29	
5		30	
6		31	
7		32	
8		33	
9		34	
10		35	
11		36	
12		37	
13		38	
14		39	
15		40	
16		41	
17		42	
18		43	
19		44	
20		45	
21		46	
22		47	
23		48	
24		49	
25		50	

Number of personal papers herein __0__.

*Book Mark :*_____

UNION ARMY. CIVIL WAR.

Also personally appeared James Donnelly and Charles Devon residents of Madison County of Jefferson State of Indiana whom I certify to be respectable and entitled to credit, and who being by me first duly sworn, say they were present and saw Elizabeth Hiner sign her name Elizabeth Hiner to the foregoing declaration and power of attorney; and they further swear that they have every reason to believe, from the appearance of the applicant and their acquaintance with her, that she is the identical person she represents herself to be: that they have been well acquainted with her and her said husband John Hiner deceased, for 8 years, and know they lived together as husband and wife, and were so reputed; in the neighborhood in which she resided that the names, ages and residence of his children as represented by her in the foregoing declaration are true as they verily believe: and also that they are the only children of said John Hiner under sixteen years of age at the time of his decease. They further declare that she has remained a widow ever since her husband's decease, and that she has not, in any manner, aided or abetted the rebellion; and that they have no interest in the presecution of this claim, and that they are not near relatives of the claimant nor relating at all in any names we cannot be mistaken as to relationship between decedent and applicant.

Signature of Witnesses,

James Donnelly
Charles Devon

Sworn to, acknowledged and subscribed, before me, this 23 day of May 1865 and I hereby certify that the contents of the foregoing declaration of claimant and affidavit of witnesses was made known to each of them before administering the oath, and that I have no interest, direct or indirect in the prosecution of this claim, and that I

Department of the Interior,

PENSION OFFICE,

_Aug 25_____, 1865.

Sir:

You are respectfully requested to furnish official evidence of the enrollment, muster, service, duty, and cause of death of _John_ _Heires_____, who was a _Pri_ in Co. ____, _16_ Regiment of ____ _Ind_ ____ Vols. reported died _Nov 4_ _1864_. _Medison Ind_

Please attach this Circular to your report, and return the same to this Office.

№. _96,054_

Respectfully, &c.

Joseph H Barrett

Commissioner.

_____

Aay &

Gen'l U. S. A.

29

am not in any way related to applicant.

Official signature,   David Phillips, clerk
                                  Jefferson Circuit Court
                                     Jefferson County

First application. If there is any thing wrong in this matter I desire to be informed of the same.

Res. Yours
John Roberts

Letter sent to Hon. Jos. H. Barrett, Com. of Pensions, Washington, D.C. January 1865, and received Jan. 18 by the Department of the Interior. 96.054. Gen 129, 671.

Feb. 20, 1866 Department sent letter to J. & R. for proof of marriage and that disease was contracted he with cins 9 & 17.

LETTER
written by attorney, John Roberts, Madison, Indiana
January 12, 1867

Hon. Jos. H. Barrett, Com. of pensions.

In reply to yours of 5 inst in reference to the claim of Elizabeth Hiner I would State that Elizabeth Hiner, mother of John Hiner and widow of John Hiner first made an application for Pension on account of service and death of her husband John Hiner No. 96054. It being impossible to show that the disease of which her husband died was contracted in the service and the time place and circumstance being to the fact that her husband went away from home and enlisted and that she could not find out what officer or other persons were present when the disease was contracted, and being to the fact that her husband gave no information to any one when he entered the Hospital to her knowledge as to where and when he

Adjutant General's Office,

Washington D. C.,
Aug 12, 1865

Sir:

I have the honor to acknowledge the receipt from your Office of application for Pension No. 96,054, and to return it herewith, with such information as is furnished by the files of this Office.

It appears from the Rolls on file in this Office, that *John Hiner* was enrolled on the 22 day of Oct, 1864, at Indianapolis in Co. the 16 Regiment of Ind Volunteers, to serve One years, ~~and during the war~~, and mustered into service as a Recruit on the 22 day of Oct 1864, at Indianapolis, in ~~Co~~ for, the 16 Regiment of Indiana Volunteers, to serve One years, ~~and during the war~~. On the Muster Roll of Co. of that Regiment, for the months of 186, he is reported

It appears from a Final Statement on file in this Office that he died in Madison Genl Hospital Madison Ind Nov. 5, 1864 of "Congestion of the Brain."

I am, Sir, very respectfully, Your obedient servant,

[signature]

Assistant Adjutant General.

The Commissioner of Pensions
Washington D C.

ACT OF JULY 14, 1862.

Elizabeth Hiner

Jefferson Co, Ind, Wid of

John Hiner

Private Co 16 Ind Vol

Died in U.S. Hospit Madison Ind Nov,
4, 1864, while in the line of his duty

Pension Office. *186*

Respectfully referred to the Adjutant
General, for official evidence of service
and death.

REJECTED.

ABANDONED.

Joseph H. Barrett

Commissioner.

Received, __May 29,__ 186 _5_

Thorn & Raluts

Madison

Ind

Attorneys

32

took sick she abandoned said claim and afterwards made application for Pension on account of death of her son John Hiner. So the best of my recollection notification was sent to the Department of the Abandonment of the Department of the Interior . . .

Department of the Interior, Pension Office with this Claim on July 27, 1867 — Rejected. Abandonment.

This office on file card made this notation: March 7, 1870. Rejection affirmed. Attorney admits that he cannot prove that the Disease was contracted in line of duty. R N

Executive Department Indiana

INDIANAPOLIS   June 15, 19 84

This Certifies That the official records of which I am the lawful custodian, on file in this office, show that   Hiner, John   *joined for duty, and was enrolled as a*   Private   *of Company (* G *)* 137th *Regiment, Indiana Volunteers at*   Madison, Indiana   *on the* 16th *day of* May *18* 64 *by* Capt. McKim *and that he was duly mustered into the Military Service of the United States at*   Indianapolis, Indiana   *on the* 26th *day of* May *18* 64 *, for the term of* one-hundred (100) *years by* Lieut. Mills *Mustering Officer*

Age: 42

Mustered out at Indianapolis, Indiana on September 21, 1864

This Certificate is given as official evidence of enlistment, service and mustered out *of* Hiner, John *of* *Company* G 137th *Regiment, Indiana Volunteers* *Witness my hand and official seal.*

STATE OF INDIANA
COMMISSION ON PUBLIC RECORDS
For the Director

     Edwin J. Howell, Director

Debbie S. Dwenger
STATE COMMISSION ON PUBLIC RECORDS
Archives Division

Chapter Four

~~~~~~

Civil War and John Heiner (1844-1862)

Elizabeth Heiner received no financial relief from the pension claim she made regarding her husband's civil war service in the army. She was with poverty in caring for five children and needed assistance. Elizabeth and John Roberts returned to the Indiana Circuit Court with an appeal for a mother's pension.

Elizabeth's son, John Heiner, was eighteen years of age when he enlisted in the Union Army at Madison, Indiana. He was a muster-in under Lieutenant Mank on March 5, 1862, in the Thirty-second Regiment, Company F, Indiana Volunteer. He was a recruit, and became a Private in the army. John was described as age eighteen, with blue eyes, dark hair, good complexion, and his height was five feet and five inches. Nativity was Germany. This is a reference for his father John Heiner (1811-1864) for John Heiner's birth was in Indiana. Occupation was confectioner. He was given this number MOC-98-324. The young soldier was sent with his regiment on active duty to the south of Alabama. John Heiner died in camp on July 15, 1862 at Huntsville, Alabama of typhoid fever at General Hospital Number Five.

Civil War, Army Regiment Thirty-two was German. Camp Murphy was opened in 1861 at Marion County, Indiana, and in the Indianapolis area. August Willich was the commanding officer. Camp Murphy had Regiments 29 and 32, and the 4th Cavalry.

During the Civil War, the Thirty-second Infantry Regiment had 171 men killed, or died from wounds. The percent of loss that was killed and died of wounds was 63.8 percent. This Thirty-second Infantry had 97 who died of disease, accidents in prison, and other incidents, and the percent of loss was 36.2.

The railroad route of Indiana from Madison to Columbus, to Indianapolis, to the north, and to the south helped to move the army men. A railroad route carried John Heiner, the Union Army Private, from his home town, Madison, Indiana to Alabama.

It was because of John Heiner, and his Civil War duty and death in the Union Army Infantry that his mother and her younger children were to have financial assistance which sustained the family at home. John was to serve a term of three years in the army but his muster-out paper was signed on March 15, 1862 at Indianapolis by Colonel Simonson. Elizabeth, the mother, and her attorney filed a mother's pension claim in the Indiana Circuit Court of Jefferson County, Indiana. The first date was July 1866 and other papers were filed in 1867, 1868 and 1869.

State of Indiana
County of Jefferson ss

Subscribed and sworn to before me David G. Phillips, Clerk of Circuit Court in and for said County and State by Elizabeth Hiner and I certify that I made known the contents of affidavit to her before she was sworn to same. And also subscribed and sworn to before me by James Donnelly and Charles Devons person whom I certify to be respectable citizens of said county and entitled to credit, and I further certify, that I am not in any manner interested in Claim of Elizabeth Hiner acknowledged execution of written power of attorney before me.

Witness my hand and Seal of parliament as made on this 6th day of July 1866.

David G. Phillips, Clerk

No. 29974 98324

ACT OF JULY 14, 1862.

Elizabeth Hiner, or Hiner,
Jefferson Co., Ind., Mother of
John Hiner, or Hiner,
Pri. Co. F, 32ᵈ Ind. Inf'y
Died at Huntsville, Ala.
July 12, 1862. Fever.

Pension Office,

—————————, 186

Respectfully referred to the Adjutant
General, for official evidence of service
and death.

Joseph H. Barrett
Commissioner.

Received, July 11 1866.

John Roberts,
Madison,
Ind,
Attorney.

State of Indiana
County of Jefferson   ss

On this 6th day of July A.D. 1866 personally appeared before me David G. Phillips, Clerk of Circuit Court in and for said County and State Elizabeth Hiner a resident of Madison in the County of Jefferson and State of Indiana aged 49 years who being first duly sworn according to law doth on her oath make the following declaration in order to obtain the benefits of the pensions made by Act of Congress approved July 14, 1862 that she is the widow of John Hiner and Mother of John Heiner who was a private of Company F Commanded by Captain Capple in the 32 Regiment of Indiana Infantry Volunteers in the war of 1861 who while in the service of the United States and in the United States that she is not in receipt of a pension under the 2 Section of the Act above mentioned or under any other Act nor has she again married since the death of her son the said John Hiner - Applicants Post office address is Madison Jefferson County Indiana and she hereby appoints John Roberts of Madison Jefferson County Indiana as her agent to apply for and receive the laws and as her attorney to prosecute said Claim and she hereby withdraws her Application for Pension on account of the death of her husband John Hiner hereafore filed. John Hiner father of deceased Private died in City of Madison on or about the 4th day of November 1864 -
they have no interest whatever in her Claim for Pension on account of death of her son, that they have been personally and intimately acquainted with applicant and family for over ten years and know that applicant was entirely dependant upon her son John Hiner of Co F 32 -Indiana Volunteer for support, that her husband John Hiner died in City of Madison Jefferson County Indiana on or about the 4th day of November 1864 he knows that said John Hiner of Co F of 32 Indiana Volunteer

38

Sir:

I have the honor to acknowledge the receipt from your Office of application for Pension No. 129671, and to return it herewith, with such information as is furnished by the files of this Office.

It appears from the Rolls on file in this Office, that John Hiner was enrolled on the 5" day of mch, 1862, at Madison Ind in Co. the, 32 Regiment of Ind Volunteers, to serve 3 years, or during the war, and mustered into service as a Prin on the 5" day of mch 1862, at Indianapolis Ind in Co. the, 32 Regiment of Ind Volunteers, to serve 3 years, or during the war. On the Muster Roll of Co. F of that Regiment, for the months of July & August 1862, he is reported John Hiner "Died at Hospital in Huntsville Ala July 12 1862," cause of death not stated

This is believed to be the soldier enquired for

I am Sir very respectfully, Your obedient servant

Ennis Buck

The Commissioner of Pensions
Washington D C

Assistant Adjutant General.

39

son of applicant died leaving no widow or children as he was never married, he knows that said Son contributed to his Mother's support by furnishing her necessaries for her support and paying her the money he earned. And Son deceased labored for affaint Donnelly at his trade shoemaking and as affiant Devon was in same shop at same time are both known of their own personal knowledge that during said time of about 3 years he gave nearly all his earnings to his Mother for her support. John Hiner husband of applicant abandoned the support of his family over six years ago and from said time until his death did not contribute at all to the support of his family as he left the City of Madison and his whereabouts until his death were not known, he was very dissipated and said applicant had no other son contributing to her support. Applicant has no Real Estate and no personal property except some household furniture a value of about fifty dollars. He is not related to applicant.

James Donnelly
Charles Devon

At another appearance in the Circuit Court of Madison, Indiana, July 1867 appears Elizabeth Hiner, attorney, John Roberts, James Donnelly, and Frederick Glass.

State of Indiana
County of Jefferson ss

We, James Donnelly and Frederick Glass resident of said County and State do hereby certify that we were formerly well and personally acquainted with Elizabeth Heiner who is Applicant for Mothers Pension No 129671 and who is the Mother of John Heiner who was late a Private in Company of the 32nd Regiment of Indiana Infantry - Volunteers in the war of 1861 - and that we were also well and personally acquainted with John Heiner, Senior, who was the husband of said Applicant and father of said soldier. We further certify that said Father and Husband John Heiner, Sr., had permanently abandoned the support of said family of Heiners in the year 1858, that since that time he did not support his family. That he has not - since returned to said family or contributed to the support of said wife the Applicant that we know the above facts from personal knowledge as we were there and are well and intimately acquainted with all of said family. And we further certify that said John Heiner, Sr. is now dead having died about the 4 of November 1864 in the service of the United States at the Hospital at Madison, Indiana.

We further certify that we know from personal knowledge that said Elizabeth Heiner has had no property of any kind whatever since her said Husband abandoned her and that she had no other means of support from the time her said husband abandoned her, than that of her said son, and we further certify that we know from personal knowledge that said soldier John Heiner, Junior did support his said Mother Elizabeth Heiner from the time of said abandonment by said Heiner, Sr. up to the time of the death of said Heiner, Junior, that he paid for all the necessary provisions for the support of his mother that prior to his enlistment he worked for James Donnelly one of affiants, and that all of his wages went for his Mothers support as the money (wages of said Soldier) was paid to his said Mother with whom he was then living.

And we further swear that said Soldier at different times sent money home to his said Mother while he was in said service that we know from personal knowledge that said Hiner, Junior was the sole support of said Elizabeth Heiner after said abandonment and that there can not be a doubt as to his paying all rents and all necessary expenses

Surgeon General's Office,

RECORD AND PENSION DIVISION,

Washington, D. C., *Apl 16th*, 186 7.

Sir:

I have the honor to inform you that *John Haines Pt*

Co. *F* , *32 "* Regiment *Ind Vol* , is reported to this

Office by Surgeon *O. L. Heinick* , as having died

July 15 , 186 2, at *G Hosttl No 2*

Huntsville of "Typhoid fever"

Very respectfully,

Your obedient servant,

BY ORDER OF THE SURGEON GENERAL:

J J Woodward

Brevet Major and Asst. Surgeon, U. S. Army.

42

for a number of years before his death and that said John Heiner, Senior abandoned the support of said family in the year 1858 and that he has not since returned or in any way contributed to Applicants support. That we have no interest whatever in this matter direct or indirect.

Subscribed and sworn 22nd day of July 1867.

James Donnelly
Frederick Glass

Madison 98325

ARREARS July 27 - 1868 and
CLAIM FOR MOTHER'S PENSION

Brief in the case of Elizabeth Heiner

John Heiner, Pri. Co. F 32. Ind. Vol. resident of Jefferson, County of State of Indiana
Post Office address, Madison, Ind.
Declaration and Identification In Due Form

PROOF EXHIBITED

Service — John Heiner. Enrolled and Mustered March 5 - 1862. John Heiner. Died. Huntsville, Ala. July 12 - 1862. By A.G.

Death — Died July 12 - 1862 at Huntsville, Ala. of typhoid fever. By S.G.

Celibacy of Soldier - Shown by credible witness.
Relationship - Shown in like manner.

Death or disability of husband — Husband abandoned family in 1858 — never returned or did any thing to support them — now dead. Died 1864.

Claimant is very poor — Son supported her by his labor — gave his earnings to her and took care of her.
Had no other support after husband abandoned her and C.

43

Loyalty — Amened.
Date of filing last evidence July 26, 1869.

Agent and his P.O. address —
John Robert. Madison, Ind.

Admitted — August 1st, 1867, to a Pension of $8.00 per month, commencing July 26, 1867.

Exd. — 26 July 1869.

A.M. Scott
Examing Clerk

DECLARATION
FOR ARREARS OF PENSION.

Under Section . . . . Act of July 1868.

State of Indiana
Jefferson County   ss:

On this 16th day of November 1868 personally appeared before me, David G. Phillips a Clerk of the Circuit Court in and for said County, Elizabeth Heiner aged 51 years, a resident of Madison State of Indiana, who being duly sworn according to law, declares that she is the identical Elizabeth Heiner to whom was granted Pension Certificate No. 98324 payable at the agency at Madison Indiana and dated Aug. 17 - 1867. That under the limitation of the Act of Congress Limiting date of Pension was denied a pension from the date of the death of her son, July 13 - 1862 to July 26 - 1867, and believing herself entitled to the same under the 6th Section of the Act, July 27th, 1868. She makes this declaration in order to secure the arrears accrued thereunder.

And for the purpose of prosecuting her claim, she hereby appoints Walter S. Roberts of Madison, State of Indiana her Attorney in fact, with full power of substitution and with authority to receive her

No. 98324

Indiana

Elizabeth Heiner

Mother of

John Heiner

Rank Private

Company "F"

Regiment 32" Ind.

Madison Agency.

Rate per month $ 8

Commencing 26 July 1867

Certificate dated 15 Aug. 1867

and sent to J. Roberts

Madison

Ind

Act 14th July, 1862.

Pension Certificate when issued, she desires all communications concerning this claim to be sent to her said attorney.

Her Post Office address is as follows Madison Indiana.

Elizabeth Heiner

Also personally appeared Frederick Glass and James Donnelly residents of Madison Indiana, persons whom I certify to be responsible and entitled to credit, and who being by me duly sworn say that they were present and saw Elizabeth Heiner sign her name to the foregoing declaration, and they further swear that they have every reason to believe, from the appearance of the applicant and their acquaintance with her that she is the identical person she represents herself to be, and that they have no interest in the prosecution of this claim.

James Donnelly
Frederick Glass

Subscribed and sworn to before me, this 16 day of November 1868, and I hereby certify that I have no interest, direct or indirect, in the prosecution of this claim and I certify that the contents of the foregoing declaration and affidavit was made known to each of said affiants before authentication.

Danil G. Phillips
Clerk

Chapter Five

~~~~~~

Mr. and Mrs. Outh had several children, and one of the daughters was Elizabeth, born in 1817. When she was a little girl, her parents left their home in Prussia, Germany in the 1820s and moved to the United States.[1] The family entered an Atlantic seaport, and lived in Pennsylvania. They had kinship in the United States for Outh arrived in America in the 1700s.

A court document dated May 23, 1865 has Elizabeth Heiner's maiden name obscurely handwritten and misspelled by a clerk of the court. The Declaration For Widow's Army Pension circuit court paper of Jefferson County, Indiana is a two page document. The following is a small portion of the document.

at _Madison_ in the State of. _Indiana_ on the _4_ day of _November_ A. D., 186_4_. She further declares that she was married to the said _John Heiner_ in the County of _Ohio_ and State of _Virginia_ on the _4_ day of _April_ in the year _1837_; that her name before her said marriage was _Elizabeth Auht_. That her husband, the aforesaid _John Heiner_ died on the day above mentioned.

Elizabeth Heiner's maiden name is certainly a four letter word. According to her daughter, Margaret, the maiden name is Outh.[2] Auht written on the court document does not appear on the United States Federal Census.

When some of the Outh family members moved west they had to cross the Allegheny Mountains. The physical features of the region made West Virginia accessible from Pennsylvania. In April 1837, Elizabeth was in Ohio County, Virginia. There Elizabeth, age twenty, married John Heiner. Elizabeth and John made their vows of matrimony in a forest among the trees, ferns, and grasses on April 4, 1837. The brothers and friends were in the forest and were witnesses to John and Elizabeth's marriage.[3]

Mr. and Mrs. John Heiner took a long journey down the Ohio River and they travelled on two boats. They saw the Virginia military reserve in Ohio. John and Elizabeth departed along the northern shore of the Ohio River about Jefferson and Clark Counties. There was a fort built earlier in the area. They settled in a place they called Hosbell, Indiana in the 1840s.[4]

Heiner Family

In a place near the Ohio River in Indiana, in 1840, the first child was born and was named George. In 1844, the second boy was born to Elizabeth and was named John. Then in 1848, according to Elizabeth, her daughter Catharine Elizabeth was born. She was called Elisa, affectionately.[5] On the 20th day of April in 1851 twins were born. Elizabeth, with her husband, named them Henry and Atha.[6] On the first day of May, 1854, the daughter, Mary, was born.

The first records on the Heiner family in Indiana may have been lost, for they have not been found. The old Courthouse of Madison, Indiana was destroyed by fire on September 12, 1853. In 1856 the family attended St. Mary's Church at Madison. The church was a beautiful house of brick on Second Street, east of Walnut. It was the German Catholic Church.

There were two fine edifices of the Roman Catholic Church built early in Madison. St. Michael's was the older building and for many years the only one in the

SISTER FRANCES DE CHANTAL   SISTER BASILISSA
SISTERS OF PROVIDENCE
ST. MARY OF THE WOODS, INDIANA

MARY HEINER WEHRLE (1855-1939)

MARGARET HEINER (1856-1923)

city of Madison. St. Michael's church had English speaking members without the foreign dialects. Later St. Patrick's Church was built of brick at North Madison. All members of the churches used the catholic cemetery, and there was also the Springdale cemetery of Madison.

John and Elizabeth attended the St. Mary's Church taking their children with them. Faith was important and so was the church. It was there that their daughter, Margaret Heiner, was baptized on the 28th day of December, 1856. Margaret was born on the 4th day of December, 1856, in Madison, Indiana. The Rite of Baptism was performed by L. Brandt and the sponsors were Wilhelm Horuff and Barbara Erwin.

The last child, a boy, was born on November 25, 1859, and was named Ferdinand. In the family there were four boys and four girls. On June 11, 1860, when the federal census taker took the family information, he gave the family dwelling enumerator Number 274, Jefferson County, Township the City of Madison, 6th Ward. Post Office at Madison, dwelling number 276.

In the 1860s, in the neighborhood of John and Elizabeth Heiner, lived a Thomas Dremidge, age 30, and his wife, Mary, age 26, both born in Ireland. They had a one year old son, William. Margaret Short, age 11, lived in the house. In another house lived Levi Estitine, age 35, a saddle maker. He was born in Pennsylvania. His wife, Elizabeth Estitine, was age 30, and born in Indiana, and her son, Emery Estitine, was born in Ohio.

The other neighbors were Edward Zeizer and wife, Catharine, both born in Germany. John Sinidlap, born in Indiana was age 31, and a druggist. Another neighbor was Samuel M. Good, a dentist, born in Indiana. His wife, Eliza, was born in Indiana. They had four children Fanny, Sarah, Blanche and Harriet. Engbert Dolde, born in Germany was age 32, was a silversmith and he lived in another house with Rosanna, age 20, and this wife had a child named Albert. There was Jacob Weber, age 46, born in Germany, as well as his wife, Margaret, age 49. In their house was Barbar Weber, age 18, who was born in Germany, and Caroline Weber, age 9, born in Indiana.[7]

On July 24, 1864 at St. Mary's Church there was a day for confirmation of the faith, in which two Heiner children participated: Henry Joseph Ferdinand Heiner, age 13, and his sister, Agatha Maria Barbara Heiner, age 13. All of the family were living together in 1864, until the departure of Elizabeth, the daughter, to north Madison. On September 1, 1864 at St. Mary's Church was the wedding of Elizabeth Heiner and Joseph Fox.

The husband, John Hiner, left home enlisted in the military service during the Civil War. He died from an illness in November of 1864 at age fifty-three. It was a difficult time for the widow. Elizabeth's friend was James Donnelly, the owner of the *Boot And Shoe* shop where she sometimes worked. He tried to help her.

John Roberts, an attorney, gave assistance to Elizabeth and became her counselor. Elizabeth Hiner applied for a pension, and was rejected on the application with husband. She applied again for the pension as a mother, and on the application with her son, John. She had to support the family, and had only what help the son Henry J. could bring home to keep the hunger away, and pay the rent. She became a seamstress. S.S. Moffet owned a dry goods store. She sewed the dresses used on the models at the store, and took in sewing.

It must have been a time of change with the family. Elizabeth did not remain in their house but moved. Her son, Henry J. became a clerk for *S.S. Moffet Company*. In 1867, the Madison Business Directory listed her as the widow of John living at the north side of the Michigan Road opposite Broadway. Henry J. was listed

51

Reissue No. 98324

Elizabeth Heiner

Mother of

John Heiner

Rank Private

Company F.

Regiment 32" Ind.

~~Kansas~~ St. Louis Agency.

Transf'd (Ex. Order May 7'77) to Chicago.

Rate per month $

Commencing 12 July 1862

~~these payments to be deducted~~

Certificate dated 2 Feby 1869

and sent to W. S. Roberts

Madison, Ind.

Act 14th July, 1862.

Book C Vol. 4 Page 283

Wurpse .... Clerk.

at the same address.[8]

Frederick Glass, age 40, was the Coffee House keeper in Madison and he became a friend and entered the court on her behalf. He lived on Third Street, on the east side of Madison. The Glass family came from Bavaria, Germany.[9]

On September 29, 1867, Elizabeth was at St. Mary's Church for the confirmation of her daughter, Maria (Mary) Heiner, age 13. The following year, in 1868, on October 25 she was at the church for the confirmation of her daughter Margaret Heiner, age 12.[10]

In 1870, on the Federal Census Record for Madison, Indiana, there is another verified report on Elizabeth and her children.

Jefferson County. City of Madison. Microfilm 593.
Post Office - Madison.
Page 75. Dwelling 545. Family No. 576. On line 14.

Heiner, Elizabeth.

Age 53. Female. White. Occupation - Seamstress. Birthplace - Prussia. Father and Mother of foreign birth.

Heiner, Henry. Age 19. Male. White. Occupation - Dry goods clerk. Birthplace - Indiana. Father and Mother of foreign birth.

Heiner, Mary. Age 16. Female. At home. Birthplace - Indiana.

Heiner, Maggie. Age 13. Female. Goes to school. Birthplace - Indiana.

Heiner, Freddie. Age 10. Male. Goes to school. Birthplace - Indiana.

Children all have father and mother of foreign birth.

Elizabeth was living with two sons and two daughters.

Margaret Heiner entered the Sisters of Providence, St. Mary of the Woods on May 28, 1872 in Vigo County, Indiana. The Catholic Order was founded in 1806 in France and began in 1840 in America. In 1875, Margaret was a teacher in the Novitiate. The nun's final vows were taken in 1879 and her religious name was Sister Basilissa. In 1882-1888 she was the Director of Novices and a member of the General Council in charge of education and she was continuously elected to the positions. For forty years she held various offices: Local Superior, Mistress of Novices, Assistant to the Superior General.

She was a founder of St. Mel's School in Chicago, Illinois. In Chicago she attended Delu University. For fifty-one years she devoted herself to the work of the schools. Almost her entire life was spent in training teachers and visiting the establishments as school examiner. She wrote a Teacher's Guide in 1899, reprinted 1914, seven publications on the heavenly *Queen* and three on the *Angels*. Sister Basilissa Heiner was a noted educator. On December 7, 1923, she died at the convent.[5]

Atha Heiner left home in 1868 or 1869. She may have joined a convent. She may have married. Her adult life is unknown.

Elizabeth Heiner Fox moved from Madison to Simpson County, Kentucky, with three children after Joseph Fox found a shop in Bowling Green in 1869.

In 1879, Elizabeth and Ferdinand, clerk for *S.S. Moffet and Sons,* lived on Second Street between Baltimore and Clay. Mrs. Heiner continued to live with a son, and had a neighbor to do the housekeeping. She worked as a seamstress. The sons, Henry J. and Ferdinand B. never married. They were very busy at the *S.S. Moffet and Sons* store. At one time the family lived across the street from the store.

On July 4, 1901, Elizabeth Heiner died at Madison, Indiana. She was age eighty-four. Indiana was her home from 1840 to July 1901. Elizabeth was laid to rest at St. Joseph's Cemetery in downtown Madison, or St. Patrick's on the hilltop. No stone marks the site. The death record is the notice recorded by the United States Pension Department.

Mary Heiner learned sewing from her mother and was very skilled in sewing. George and Anna Wehrle who lived next door to the Heiners had five sons and a daughter. George, age 23, and Charles, age 18, were dry goods clerks in 1870. Fred, age 16, was a dry goods store clerk. Mary Heiner married one of these young men. Mary had a very short but happy married life. Death took her husband.

Several years passed and Mary Wehrle received permission to enter the Sisters of Providence on September 24, 1888. The Bishop of Vincennes issued an Indult for her to join the religious community of Sisters. Mary became Sister Frances de Chantal. Her profession was in 1891 and her vinal vows in 1899.

Sister Frances de Chantal taught sewing at the Academy for some years. After that she became Sacristan for the church of the Immaculate Conception and did all the sewing of linens and vestments. She died at age 83 on January 5, 1939 at St. Mary of the Woods near Terra Haute city.[6]

Old letters written by Henry and Margaret to Elizabeth Fox leave messages about the Heiner family. The gleam on the Heiner families are from old letters written by children living with their mother, Elizabeth Heiner. The letters had to have historical interpretation on the children's writings. The messages were the following:

"They married in a forest without writing . . . Folks on two boats . . . Cross to Kentucky two times . . .

We know about brothers . . . Came from Way with nee *(interpreted as Wayne)* . . . Our relatives in Bartholomew *(interpreted as County of Indiana)* . . . They wrote with Bartholomew on the mail . . . Uncle Oliver will help us . . . We have some hunger . . . Atha is thin and pitiful, she gets more bonbon nourishers than us . . . We have to do things to keep hunger away . . . Folks old in born and there are dear *(interpreted as Dearborn County)* . . . I knew Elisa a little time *(Henry was age 13 when Elizabeth married and sisters were much younger)* . . . Our mother over-wrote the words *(she used more alphabet letters than spelled in an english work)* . . . living all right."[11]

Actually, Elizabeth used perfect German-English grammar when she wrote.

In 1870, Elizabeth had three grandchildren: Theodore, George, and Francesca. The daughter, Elizabeth Fox, moved with three of the children to Kentucky, and lived at Franklin town.[12]

Chapter Six

~ ~

On September 1, 1864, Joseph G. Fox married Elizabeth Heiner at St. Mary's Church in Madison, Indiana. The marriage was performed according to the Rite of the Roman Catholic Church with a priest, L. Brandt, officiating, in the presence of John Lang and Frances Schmidt, as witnesses. Mr. and Mrs. John Heiner, and their children, and friends were present at the wedding.

Life of Joseph G. Fox 1832-1888

Joseph George Fox was born on the 2nd day of April, 1832, and was a native of Baden, Germany. He went to school with his brothers and sisters. At age twenty he left home with a brother or a friend and went to a sailing port and emigrated from Harire de Grace on the 17th day of September, 1852, and arrived at New York on the 28th day of October, 1852.[1] He had a brother in America.

Joseph Fox left New York traveling on roads across the country. He reached the Ohio River, and like most travelers took a boat to Indiana with the intent to join the German community. Joseph Fox settled at Madison, Indiana in the home of Peter Weber, and went to baking bread at the Union Bakery. A George Fox from Bavaria, Germany had settled in 1846 in Madison, Indiana, and he may have been a relative.

Joseph Fox applied for his naturalization in 1854 or 1855. The naturalization paper follows: "Joseph Fox an alien, a native of Baden, Germany, aged about 32

Joseph Fox an alien, a native of Baden... Germany, aged about 32 years bearing allegiance to the King of Baden, who migrated from Baden Dukedom the 14 day of September 1862, and arrived at New York on the 28 day of October 1862, and who intends to reside within the jurisdiction and under the government of the United States, Tount, Indiana, and he makes report of himself for naturalization and declares on oath that it is bona fide his intention to become a citizen of the United States of America and to forever renounce and abjure all allegiance and fidelity to every foreign Prince, Potentate, state or sovereignty whatever and particularly to the King of Baden to whom he is now a subject.

JOSEPH FOX NATURALIZATION 1854-1855.

years bearing allegiance to the King of Baden, who emigrated from Harire de Grace on the 17th day of September 1852, and arrived at New York on the 28th day of October 1852, and who intended to reside within the jurisdiction and under the Government of the United States, to wit: Indiana, and he makes report of himself for naturalization and declares an oath that it is bona fide his intention to become a citizen of the United States of America and to forever renounce and abjure all allegiance and fidelity to every foreign Prince Potentate, State or Sovereignty whatever and particularly to the King of Baden to whom he is now a subject.[3]"

Joseph Fox was a baker with Union Bakery. At this bakery, Weber, Fox and Pappots worked together making, baking, supplying and selling bread in the town of Madison.

On June 15, 1860, A.G. Reed, Assistant Marshall and Federal Census Taker, found at the dwelling 311 of the 7th Ward, in Madison, Indiana of Jefferson County the Union Bakery. At the dwelling was Peter Weber, age 28, born in France. Union Bakery had a real estate value of $2,500.00. Weber had a personal property value of $500. Charlotte Weber, the wife was age 17, and was born in Germany. Lewis Weber, age two, was born in Indiana. M.A. Henrietta Weber, age 59, female, and widow, was born in France. Joseph Fox, age 28, a baker, was born in Germany. Henry Pappots, age 21, baker, was born in Germany.[4]

In The Madison Ward of this neighborhood was John Todd, age 77, farmer with wife, Nancy, 77, Margaret, 40, Caroline Morris, 35 widow. Hohn H. Morris, age two. William G. Wharton, age 58, and his family. He was a pork packer.

A Civil War military record could not be found for this Joseph Fox. He made breads during the Civil War.

FEDERAL CENSUS OF INDIANA

Peter Weber and Family
Joseph Fox
Henry Pappots

UNION BAKERY

June 15 , 1860 , Madison, Indiana

It was the only food prepared by him until he met a confectioner, George Heiner, and his young sister, Elizabeth. He then baked sweet breads, and did sugar confectionary cooking.

Joseph and Elizabeth Fox lived in north Madison, and attended St. Michael's Catholic Church. Children were born to the parents in 1865, 1867, 1868 and 1870. In 1869 Joseph was in search of a shop of his own, and took a trip to Clarksville, Indiana. An old letter to Elizabeth, written April 13, 1869, follows:

"Dear Wife. I have received your letter last Saturday and the news you give me affected me very much. I felt like if we had lost one of our already nursed ones, tough, God thanks that you got over so safe, it might cost your life, no wonder that I felt so uneasy about you all and it breaks almost my heart to know that we are in such circumstances. I do not know when I will be back exactly. I found out this old fellow to be a great rascal and don't know wether to trust him to move here and depend on him. I think that I can get another shop . . . soon here and . . . for romance . . . I have to wait till next fall or maybe sooner. I sent you money with this and hope this will in better health.

My love to You All
Your affectionate husband,

Jos. Fox"

The letter shows that Joseph Fox was not always at home. He had to travel where the people's gatherings were that needed a special cook. "He was a high class baker and candy-maker. Made all cakes for mayors, governors and rich weddings and was noted to be the best. He got jobs in Kentucky, New York, St. Louis and elsewhere to bake fine cakes. He decided to travel no more and so he settled down in Franklin" in June 1870.[5]

On August 16, 1870, S. Simpson, Assistant Marshall of number one voting precinct called at the dwelling of the Fox family and took the census. He wrote, mistakenly, Joseph Cox instead of Joseph Fox on the census on lien 15, dwelling 117. Federal Census Schedule One, Inhabitants in Subdivision District Number 150, in the county of Simpson, State of Kentucky. Post office, Franklin, Kentucky. This Fox family is Joseph Cox's listing on the 1870 Federal Census of Franklin. He wrote, "Joseph, age 38, Baker and Confectioner, $300 value real estate, born Germany. Elizabeth, age 28, born Kentucky. Theodore, age 5, born Indiana. George, age 3, born Indiana. Frances, age 2, born Indiana. Charles, age 4 months, born Indiana. Scott Delphis, age 14, female, born Virginia." The county tally was with the enumerated inhabitants of 4,519 in Simpson County, Kentucky in 1870.

A neighbor on the road in this Ward of Franklin was George Patterson, age 38, born in Virginia. He retailed dry goods. His wife was Sarah, age 27, and one child, May, age 4. There were three adults of other names in the house. There was Samuel Nahm, age 35, retailer of boots and shoes. He was born in Germany. Wife was Fanny, age 23. The child Atama was eleven months. Susan Sanders, age 9, lived in the house.[6]

When Joseph Fox and family moved to Franklin, Kentucky "he put all his money in a nice bakery shop in Franklin. He had no customers come in. A man came in and talked to Joseph and told him people were afraid to come in his store. Man there before him had smallpox and died there."[7] People were scared of smallpox. The shop was located on the Franklin town square. In addition to this, the farmers' wives baked their own bread and foods.

FEDERAL CENSUS. Supervisor's District No. 2. Enumeration District No. 241. Page 241. SCHEDULE 1. Inhabitants in FRANKLIN in the County of SIMPSON, State of KENTUCKY enumerated by me on the 15th day of June, 1880. Henry Brivard, Enumerator. Original copy on Fox family.

63

Joseph Fox "sold to other bakers, ovens and everything was moved out and he started on the road again, usually gone six months or a year then home a little while then gone again."[8]

He could not settle down. He worked from his home, and continued to travel for the public gatherings and events where he could give service with food.

When he was away from home he wrote letters to Elizabeth. Her letters to him affected him much when there was sickness in the family. A son, Charles, died in 1871. Joseph Fox ordered a burial lot in the Greenlawn Catholic portion of the cemetery. This parcel became the family burial yard of their hometown.[9] Daughter, Francesca Maria Fox, age 5, died in 1873. Baby, Robert in 1878. Both died of epidemic diseases common to children then. Elizabeth's letters also affected Joseph with happines for five more children were born at their home in Franklin, Kentucky.

On June 15, 1880, Federal Census, Page 24, Franklin, Simpson County, Kentucky appears Joseph Fox and family. Dwelling visitation number 225 of the census taker, and count of people in houses 254. Joseph Fox, age 48, white, male, baker confections, born Bavaria. Elizabeth, age 38, wife, keeping house, place of birth Kentucky. The census listed four sons and two daughters.[10] With this census it was determined that the place of birth by choice of Joseph and Elizabeth was now given. Elizabeth Fox was born in Hosbell, Indiana, but she has chosen Kentucky. Joseph Fox was a native of Baden. Perhaps his family had some connecion with Bavaria, Germany, or the boundary of the regions had changed. For his birthplace we can place Baden, a region of Germany, which was near the Bavaria region. Henry Brivard was the enumerator on this 1880 census.

The parents of Joseph Fox were both in Germany. It appears they did not come to America. The name of

64

Certificate of Death for Joseph Fox certified from copy :

County Davidson , Roll No. M-2 , Book 1874-1889 , Page 92 ,
Death , Certificate # 510 . Tennessee State Library and Archives , and
same record as with Vital Statistics of Tennessee.

Original record as it appears on 1888 list of deaths , Davidson County, Tenn.

Date *1888* Name

June

510 29 *Fox Joseph*

Year	Sex Color	Married	Nativity
Age			
56		*W W Germany*	

Residence   Ward   Cause of Death   By Whom Certified

27 *Putman 13 Malarial Fever*   *J. M. Coyle*

Cemetery   Undertaker

Franklin S. N.C. Cornelius

65

Certificate of Marriage

CHURCH OF

St. Mary
Madison, Indiana 47250

✳ This is to Certify ✳

That __Joseph Fox__

and __Elizabeth Heiner__

✳ Were Lawfully Married ✳

on the ____1st____ day of __September 1864__

According to the Rite of the Roman Catholic Church

and in conformity with the laws of the State of

Rev. __L. Brandt__

officiating, in the presence of __John Lang__

and __Frances Schmidt__ Witnesses, as appears

from the Marriage Register of this Church.

Dated __September 4, 1984__

_____John L. Fink_____ Pastor.

INDIANA MARRIAGE LICENSE

OF JOSEPH FOX AND ELIZABETH HINER.

Fox was always their name in Germany. Fox is a surname that originated in England long ago. Germany had many families with the name of Fox.

About 1883, Joseph Fox and family moved to Nashville, Tennessee. Joseph Fox and sons, Theodore and George, found work as baker confectioners in Nashville. It was a growing town with new buildings, and the Cumberland River running through the district. Theodore and George became the town's candy-makers.

Joseph continued to travel. He went in 1888 to New Orleans, Louisiana to work. A seaport town with mosquitoes. He became sick there. He did not get well but went home to his wife.[11] Joseph G. Fox died with malaria on June 29, 1888 at Nashville, Tennessee. Elizabeth and his sons took him to the Fox burial yard in Greenlawn Cemetery at Franklin, Kentucky.[12]

Life of Elizabeth Heiner Fox 1842-1919

Elizabeth Fox was the daughter of John and Elizabeth Heiner. She was born December 15th in the 1840s, in Indiana.[13] She lived with her family at Madison, Indiana and went to school there. Elizabeth Heiner attended St. Mary's Church of the Catholic faith. Elizabeth was married there on September 1, 1864 to Joseph G. Fox.

Mr. and Mrs. Joseph Fox moved to north Madison, and attended St. Michael's Church. Elizabeth had the rite of confirmation at St. Patrick's Church on August 24, 1864.

Elizabeth Fox was wife, mother, housekeeper, cook, and candy-maker. She lived in Madison, Indiana of Jefferson County from 1855 to 1869. Elizabeth lived in Franklin, Kentucky of Simpson County from 1869 to 1883, and she lived in Nashville, Tennessee of Davidson County from 1883 to January 1919.

Elizabeth Heiner Fox was the mother of twelve

ELIZABETH HEINER FOX

children. Joseph G. Fox was the father.

Theodore Joseph Fox, b. May 26, 1865, Madison, Indiana; d. 1930s in Missouri.

George Fox, b. February 22, 1867, Madison, Indiana; d. February 23, 1942, Nashville, Tennessee.

Francesca Maria Fox, daughter, b. May 13, 1868, Madison, Indiana. She died June 28, 1873, Franklin, Kentucky.

Arthur Fox, b. 1869, Madison, Indiana; d. 1926,

Cincinnati, Ohio.

Charles Fox, b. April 13, 1870, Madison, Indiana, he was called Charley; d. July 28, 1871, Franklin, Kentucky.

Henrietta Fox was called Nettie Fox Hager, b. April 10, 1872, Franklin, Kentucky. She was baptized on September 22, 1872. She died February 5, 1954 in Cartland, Tennessee.

Henry Albert Fox, b. February 15, 1874, Franklin, Kentucky, he was called Albert. He died November 12, 1951, Woodmont, Connecticut. Baptized March 15, 1874.

Eugene Fox, b. May 26, 1875, Franklin, Kentucky; d. October 22, 1876, Franklin, Kentucky. Baptized August 15, 1875.

Margaritam Helenam Fannie Fox, b. 1877, Franklin, Kentucky; d. about 1903, Nashville, Tennessee. Margaritam was called Fannie Fox.[14]

Robert Fox, b. March 26, 1878; d. August 4, 1878, Franklin, Kentucky.

Bernard Joseph Fox was called Ben Fox, and he was born March 22, 1879, Franklin, Kentucky. Bernard was baptized on March 29, 1879. He died October 28, 1945, Madison, Tennessee.

Joseph Edward Fox was called Joe Fox, and he was born December 1, 1880. He died July 25, 1942, Nashville, Tennessee.[15]

Joseph and Elizabeth Heiner Fox attended St. Mary's Church of Franklin, Kentucky. This church was a mission parish of Sacred Heart Church in Russellville, Kentucky. It was there they carried their children to the church for baptisms. According to an old German custom, the children were baptized and their names were made part of the church records.

Carrolum Josephum baptized 6/19/1870
Antonium Josephum baptized 7/2/1971

Certificate of Baptism

CHURCH OF

St. Michael's

Madison, In. 47250

This is to Certify

That _Theodore Joseph Fox_

Child of _Joseph G. Fox_

and _Elizabeth Fox_

born in _Madison, Indiana_

on the _26th_ day of _May_ _1865_

Was Baptized

on the _11th_ day of _June_ _1865_

According to the Rite of the Roman Catholic Church

by the Rev. _H. Dupontavice_

the Sponsors being _Bernard Wohl_

and _Francisca Okle_ as appears

from the Baptismal Register of this Church.

Dated _September 12, 1984_

John L. Fink Pastor.

Certificate of Baptism

CHURCH OF

St. Mary's

Madison, In. 47250

This is to Certify

That *Francesca Maria Fox*

Child of *Joseph Fox*

and *Elisabeth Heiner*

born in *Madison, In. ,*

on the *13th* day of *May* *1868*

Was Baptized

on the *31st* day of *May* *1868*

According to the Rite of the Roman Catholic Church

by the Rev. *L. Brandt*

the Sponsors being *Henricus Heiner*

and *Catharina Eichelbrenner* as appears

from the Baptismal Register of this Church.

Dated *September 12, 1984*

John L. Fink Pastor.

Madison April 15 1899

Dear Sister
this letter came To madison
as you see on the Envelope.
there are same Foxes out
in georgetown. they got
it out of the Post Office
and Opened it I dont know
how many hands it went
through. Mrs Betz took it
out of the Post Office and
thought it was in care of
her husband the little Gloss
Boy brought it to me
in the store it say dont
say how much money
was in it. there was 9
Dollars in it when we got
it.

I write soon
and let us know
if you got it
or not
        Your Brother
        H Hiner

Letter written to Elizabeth Hiner Fox by H. Hiner 1899.

73

Henrietta Jilia Josephi baptized 9/22/1872
Henry Albert baptized 3/15/1874
Eugene John baptized 3/29/1875
Bernardum Josephum baptized 3/29/1879
Edwardum Josephum baptized 12/18/1880

Elizabeth Fox was the mother of nine sons and three daughters. Four of her young children died from diseases in Franklin, Kentucky. The family attended St. Mary's Church. On the federal census, Elizabeth's occupation was listed as housekeeper.

Joseph, her husband, was a good confectioner baker, and that is why all the boys came to be candy-makers, with the exception of Bernard and Joseph E. On June 29, 1888, Elizabeth was the widow of Joseph G. Fox.[16]

With the estate of her husband, Elizabeth purchased two properties. On October 23, 1888, for $625, she bought from William and Ellen Griffith, land lot number two with house in Millers Subdivision, Wetwares Plan. The lot was 50 feet front by 165 feet back at 226 Spring Street in Edgefield District of east Nashville, Tennessee. This property became her home. It was a small wooden frame house of three rooms. There was one large parlor room occupying half of the house, and at night it was used as a sleeper's room. One bedroom and a kitchen occupied the other half of the house. A porch was across the front of the house.[17]

On November 20, 1889, Elizabeth Fox paid $1,040.00 to John H. and Ellen J. Mathews for part of Lot number 72 in Harris addition of Edgefield. The deed to this house and lot was located on Joseph Street, only a few street blocks away from Spring Street. The size of the lot was 39 feet, thence east 150 feet, thence north 39 feet, and to west line 150 feet.[18] In this house the older sons lived; Theodore, George, Arthur and Albert. They were candy-makers in the house.

R–1091.

GENERAL LAW

PENSIONER DROPPED

United States Pension Agency.

28556. *Dropped*

Chicago, Ill.,

June 11 1904

Certificate No. 98324

Class Mothers

Pensioner Elizabeth Heiner

Soldier John

Service F. 32" Ind.

The Commissioner of Pensions.

SIR: I have the honor to report that the above-named pensioner who was last paid at $ 12, to 4 July 1901 has been dropped because of death July 4, 1901.

Very respectfully,

J. Merriam

United States Pension Agent.

NOTE.—Every name dropped to be thus reported at once, and when cause of dropping is death, state date of death when known.

75

Elizabeth sometimes helped the younger children with the candy craft by dipping and swirling chocolate and other coating ingredients on candied fruits and nuts at her house.

Margaritam Helenam Fannie Fox married and died about age 26, and she had no children. Elizabeth usually had two or three younger members of the family living with her at the house. Joseph Edward Fox and his bride, Valley, lived with her from 1909 until about 1916. In these years she told many stories to Joseph and Valley about her husband and the sons and daughters. Those stories of family personal history that Elizabeth Fox told helped to give substance to the Fox history.

Elizabeth died of heart failure on January 7, 1919 in Nashville, Tennessee. The Fox sons and daughter carried her back to Franklin, Kentucky to rest beside Joseph G. Fox. She left this will:

"I, Elizabeth Fox, do this day Nov. 16, 1917, execute this my last will and testament, I devise that all my just debts be paid.

My funeral expenses not to exceed two hundred and fifty dollars, $250.00. I wish to be buried with Mass and taken to Franklin, Kentucky, and buried by the side of my husband.

The house and lot on Spring St. and the house and lot on Joseph Ave. and the household furniture to be sold and the proceeds equally divided among my seven children Nettie Fox Hager, Albert Fox, Arthur Fox, Ben Fox, Theodore Fox, George Fox and Joe Fox.

To Nettie Fox Hager I give my clothes the silver goblet, silver butter dish and my picture in the oval frame and my mother's picture.

To Lottie Fox I give the china dishes, picture clinging to the Cross, and my sister's picture.

To Valley Fox I give my husband's picture in the small frame, the green and lavender comfort and the light weight feather bed.

To May Fox I give the Life of Christ unbound, my picture in the gilt frame and the crazy quilt.

To little Maria my grand daughter I give the shell vase.

To Emma Fox I give my husband's picture in the large frame, the silk quilt and my brother's picture in the soldier's uniform.

My son George Fox I wish to have seventy five dollars more than the rest and my son Theodore I wish to have half as much as is the share of the others.

If he tries to break the will he is to get nothing.

The quilts, blankets, sheets and comforts that are remaining are to be divided among my daughter, Nettie and my daughters in law.

Signed. Mrs. Elizabeth Fox.

Witnessed by: Mrs. Kak Hamberg

Mrs. Florence Crawford

Nov. 16, 1917, Nashville, Tennessee.

I, Elizabeth Fox wish to add this codicil to my last will and testament.

I wish to have an inscription (My name and the date of my death) inscribed on the monument now erected on my lot in Franklin, Kentucky over my husband's grave. The expense of this to be taken out of the proceeds derived from the sale of my property before the division is made among my children.

I wish to appoint my daughter Nettie Fox Hager to attend to this and see that it is done the way I want it.

Signed. Mrs. Elizabeth Fox

Witnessed by: Mrs. Florence Crawford
Mrs. Kak Hemberger
Dec. 16, 1917, Nashville, Tennessee.[19]

The Davidson County, Tennessee Superior Court wrote a paper in response to the application of the administrators for approved Letters of Administration.

To B.J. Fox and Mrs. Nettie Hager, a citizen of Davidson County: It appearing to the Court that Mrs. Elizabeth Fox has died, leaving a written will which has been duly proven in open court, and application being made by you to have Letters of Administration with the will granted to you on the estate of the said Mrs. Elizabeth Fox deceased, and you having qualified according to law, and the Court having ordered that letters issue:

These are therefore, to empower you, the said B.J. Fox and Mrs. Nettie Hager to enter upon the execution of said will and take into your possession all the property, and to make to the next Court, or within ninety days from the date hereof a perfect inventory thereof and make due collection of all debts, and after paying all the just demands against the estate, and settling up the business according to law, you will pay over and deliver the property and effects that may remain in your hand and do all other things that may be required, according to the provision of said will, and the law of the land. Herein fail not.

Witness, Romains Hailey, Clerk of said Court, at office, this 31 day of January 1919, and the 143 year of American Independence.

Romains Hailey, Clerk
W.E. Chadwell, D.C.

Chapter Seven

God has some special purpose for everyone on the face of the earth, and each person is called by a special name. That special name is usually the birth given name, and also the legal name. Although some people are called by shortened names, and a few people change their names. The Fox family children had name changes, but never was the last name changed except by marriage of the daughters.

The children, Francesca, Charley, Eugene and Robert, in the Fox family, were born and loved and laid to rest at an early age in Franklin, Kentucky. Six sons and one daughter survived Elizabeth Heiner Fox, who was laid to rest in Kentucky. Theodore was born on May 26, 1865, and George Fox was born on February 22, 1867. Baptismal certificates of St. Michael's Catholic Church verify the births of the first and second sons in Madison, Indiana. Francesca Maria Fox was born on May 31, 1868. On that day, a visiting priest to St. Mary's Church came to the Fox home, and later in the day baptized the infant girl.[1]

Joseph Fox had some reason to think that an opportunity offered itself in the south, perhaps an opportunity and place to have a shop of his own. Joseph and Elizabeth, two small boys and a year old girl moved from Madison, Indiana, to Franklin, Kentucky in 1869. They crossed the Ohio River by boat, and made a trip across Kentucky from the northern to the southern part, for reconstruction work after the Civil War led some people, such as Joseph Fox, to new lives and new locations.

Theodore and George entered the Franklin School

and were educated there. At home they were also educated in a craft by watching their parents as cooks and candy-makers. It is likely that the parents had a garden in the yard of their rented home, located near the community square.

The 1870s were busy years for Elizabeth. Joseph spent time at home for romance with Elizabeth, and it was a good time. Elizabeth was pregnant in the 1870s with Charley, Arthur, Henrietta, Henry Albert, Eugene, Fannie, Robert and Bernard. She gave birth in 1870, 1871, 1872, 1874, 1875, 1877, 1878 and 1879. At St. Mary's Church, the sponsors for the baptisms were Margaret M. Murphy, 1870. Thomas Cody, and Maria Anna McManus, 1871. Gregarius Duttlinger and Sophia Duttlinger, 1872. Margaret Murphy, 1874. John Walsh and Mary Murphy, 1875. Margarita Anna Murphy, 1877. Joseph Traughber and Maria Traughber, 1880. The Reverend H. Mertens baptized three Fox children in 1870, 1871, 1872.

Reverend W. Bourke baptized the Fox children in 1874 and 1875. Reverend Thomas F. Tierney baptized the children in 1876 and 1880. St. Mary's Church was a missionary parish of the Sacred Heart Church at Russellville, Kentucky in Logan County.[2] The church rite of baptism was performed one more time for the twelfth child. Edwardum Josephum Fox, who was born on the first day of December 1880. He was baptized on the eighteenth day of that month.[3]

Keeping hunger away was a job. Also nursing the young children was demanding. The older boys in school came in contact with communicable childhood diseases and became ill. Sometimes only one young child lacked enough immunity to combat an infectious germ, and they became sick and infected another. The toll was hard on the very young children. Elizabeth and Joseph watched over death in 1871, 1873,

1876 and 1878 and lost four children.

Joseph had to travel for his specialty work of confectionery cooking, and Elizabeth was often left alone with the children. She had two sisters who visited her at times. A few individuals in the church, school and neighborhood were her friends. In their minds they must have thought there was a better place for the older children. Joseph considered the future for his growing sons, Theodore and George. Rather than have Theodore leave home, a decision was made to move. In 1883, Joseph Fox and family moved from Franklin, Kentucky, to the town of Nashville, Tennessee. It was a larger town, and site of the State Capitol.

In east Nashville, the children grew and attended the local school. Theodore and George left school and went to work making confections, and sold them in the community. It was a time of progress. The building of the bridge over the Cumberland River connected the east and west of Nashville. A site on a hill at the west side of the bridge became a business location. Farmers gathered there with their products for public sale. It was an open market for farm vendors. There were peddlers. The people with food and those with like wares made exchanges among themselves for their own personal needs.

It was at this hilltop site and open market that the Fox boys were confectionery sellers, the best in town. They hitched a horse to a wagon, crossed the bridge, and sold at the open market from the back of a wagon on the weekends. In the 1920s the horse-wagon gave way to the automobile. There were more people and houses, and they went to the open market for food. This changed the look at the site. The farmers and peddlers then showed their produce and sold from the back of trucks or on tables and stands.

At this hilltop site a few old houses were torn down.

In their place was built the large courthouse building of Nashville. Commercial buildings were built across the street to the south, and shops opened. One of the first indoor buildings to hold food was built there. Elizabeth Fox loaned money to Theodore, and with his brother, George, he moved into one of the shops on the Nashville Square. Theodore and George made candies in this confectionary shop, and managed the shop for ten years.

The younger brothers finished school and moved to Elizabeth's second house. There they became confectioners making candies at the Joseph Street house. It was called the cooking house. They were candy suppliers to the store. As a brother became older he had to help with selling, and took his turn going to the open market. He could fill in at the store in the absence of Theodore or George who also traveled as sweet specialty cooks. The opportunity, adventure and travels led these men to other places.

Theodore Fox married late in life, and had no children. He was working and living in Missouri when he died about 1932.

George Joseph Fox was the son who helped his mother, Elizabeth Heiner Fox; he was a boarder with Elizabeth after the boys left home and provided her with some support. George was the father image to the younger brothers and sisters after 1888. The young brothers, Bernard and Joseph called him father. He acted in the position of father. In Nashville, George lived the longest at the home place on Spring Street.

Later, after the house was sold on Spring Street, George traveled to Ohio, Illinois and Kentucky, working and living in these places for about twelve years. He, like his brothers, Theodore, Albert, and Arthur, went north to obtain work. George never married. He visited the brothers and their wives. When he was older, he lived at Nashville, Tennessee. Although

GEORGE   FOX

very ill on February 22, 1942, he was aware of his seventy-seventh birthday; and two brothers were with him. Bernard Fox and Joseph Fox and their wives were at his bedside when he died on February 23, 1942. On a cold day the brothers and wives carried him to Franklin, Kentucky for burial in the Fox yard at the cemetery.

Arthur Fox

May 28, 1871 was the birthday of Arthur Fox. He was given the name Antonium Josephum at his baptism on July 2, 1871. His brother, Charley, was baptized June

I HEREBY CERTIFY THE ABOVE TO BE A TRUE AND CORRECT COPY OF THE ORIGINAL
RECORD ON FILE IN THIS OFFICE. (NOT VALID UNLESS COUNTERSIGNED BY STATE
REGISTRAR.)

COMMISSIONER

STATE OF TENNESSEE
DEPARTMENT OF PUBLIC HEALTH
NASHVILLE 3

APR -5 1962

Certificate of Elizabeth Elisa Hiner Fox

84

ARTHUR FOX

19, 1870 at St. Mary's Church where Arthur and all the younger Fox children were baptized. He was a young man when he left his mother's house at 226 Spring Street, and moved in with his brothers on Joseph Street. There Arthur learned to cook and make candy. He became a confectioner and joined his brothers in the trade.

Arthur Joseph Fox went to Ohio to work, and made a home in Cincinnati, Ohio. Arthur Fox married Emma K. Hirschmiller in 1912 in Ohio. Emma was born August 20, 1886, the daughter of Elizabeth and William Hirschmiller of Ohio. To this union was born a son on March 13, 1913, Arthur Joseph Fox II.

Arthur, the father, was a candy-maker, and an employee of the *Puritan Store*. He died on September 3, 1927 in Cincinnati at age fifty-six. Emma Fox made her home in Cincinnati, and remained single until her last day, March 18, 1959 in north Miami, Florida, at her sister's place.[5]

Brothers and Sisters

Robert W. Fox died at age four months in 1878. There were no vaccines and medicines readily available for children's diseases in those days.

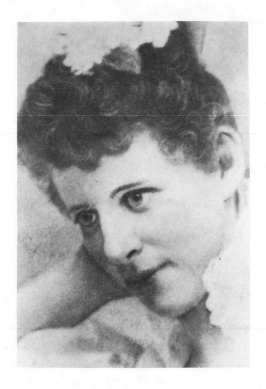

HENRIETTA FOX HAGER

Henrietta Jilia Fox was born on the 12th day of September, 1872. She was a healthy and smart child, and learned well in school. She attended Vanderbilt Dental School in Nashville. It was there she met Andrew

J. Hager, Doctor of Dental Science. Dr. Hager was divorced and had two sons. She married him in Nashville after she finished Dental School.

Henrietta became Nettie Hager, a shortened name her husband liked. She assisted Dr. Hager in his practice at Hartsville, Tennessee, where they made their home. Andrew died about 1932. Nettie stayed with her brother Bernard Fox until she became elderly. Then she moved to Chestnut Hill Sanitarium in Cartland, Tennessee, staying until the time of her death, Febrary 23, 1954. She was buried beside Andrew Hager in Hartsville, Tennessee.

When Henrietta was five years old, her sister, **Margaritam Helenam Fox** was born on the 31st day of October, 1876. She was baptized at St. Mary's Church according to the rite of the Roman Catholic Church on the eighteenth day of February, 1877. She stayed at home with Elizabeth and was a companion to Henrietta and her mother. She was an emotional person. Margaritam was called Fannie Fox. Henrietta spoke about her sister, but the brothers never spoke much about her. Later, when she was grown and the family was living in Nashville, she married. She died when she was about twenty-six years of age. She left no children.[6] In 1876, the year Fannie was born, a brother, Eugene Fox died on October 22, 1876 at Franklin. He was one year and five months old with a birthday on May 26th.

There was another brother, **Albert Henry Fox,** born February 13, 1874 in the Kentucky home in Simpson County. He had many children in the household which helped care for him and played with him. Albert went to school in Nashville. When he became an adult he followed the interest of his brothers and became a candy-maker. he took his first trip with a brother leaving Nashville, and went farther north than any of the Fox brothers. Albert traveled to New York

87

and Connecticut. He went to Bridgeport, Connecticut to work in a candy-making factory as a confectioner.

Albert Fox married Mae Elizabeth Hoyt on January 22, 1912, in New York City. She came to America in 1897 arriving at the port of Boston, Massachusetts. Mae Elizabeth Hoyt was born on June 12, 1894 in Bagelstown, County Carlow of Ireland. Her father, William Hoyt, died shortly before her birth. Her mother, Marianne Tierney Hoyt, died at her birth.[7]

Albert and Mae Fox made their home in Bridgeport, Connecticut. They had three children: Marie, Dorothy and William. Mae Fox died at age 50, on September 10, 1944 in Bridgeport. Albert Fox died at age 77, on November 12, 1951 at the hospital in Woodmont, Connecticut, in County New Haven. They practiced the Catholic faith. There was a gathering at St. Michael's yard.

The eleventh child, **Bernard Joseph Fox,** was born on the 22nd day of March, 1879. He was baptized Bernardum Josephum Fox on March 29, 1879. Bernard did not follow his brothers in the confectionery work but worked as a laborer, and then became a farmer. In 1923, Bernard and Charlotte Fox purchased one hundred and forty-nine acres of property on Neely Bend Road in Madison, Tennessee, of Davidson County. There they made their home. It was a place of southern charm near the Cumberland River bend. Bernard Fox had married Charlotte Fanny Sanders in 1906 in Nashville, Tennessee.

Bernard was called Ben Fox and he was an enterprising businessman. On the Fox farm he operated a dairy and nursery on a portion of the farm land. In 1910, Bernard and Charlotte Fox founded the *B.J. Fox and Son Bottle Company,* First Avenue, Nashville. The business was located in the second building on First Avenue, north, near the corner at the bridge crossing the

BERNARD J. FOX

Cumberland River on the west side, and continued in
that location until 1954. The building later was torn
down for city redevelopment. Charlotte Fox managed
the office of this business. In the family, she was known
as "Lottie" Fox. Mrs. Fox died on September 20, 1954,
at home. Interment of Mr. and Mrs. Bernard Fox was at
Springhill Cemetery of Madison, Tennessee.

Joseph E. Fox

The last child accepted the name Joseph Edward
Fox, although family members and others called him
Joe Fox. Joseph Edward spent all his life in Nashville,
Tennessee except for two years in Franklin, and three
years in Newport, Kentucky. He attended the local

JOSEPH EDWARD FOX   VALLEY SCHIEFER FOX

school in the Edgefield District, the only school in existence. The nearest church to the Fox family home at 226 Spring Street was St. Columba Church on Main Street near south Fifth Street. In 1890 the Pastor was Rev. E. Gazzo.

When Joseph E. Fox was a young man he began work in the *Joy Florist Shop* and worked there five years. Then the railroad trains interested Joseph. He became a railroad worker at the Nashville Terminal. Joseph E. Fox was employed at the *Louisville and Nashville Railroad Company* for thirty-five years.

A train took him to Newport, Kentucky, where he also worked. One day he went into the *Schiefer Inn* there for a meal. Valley Schiefer was the waitress. Joseph took more meals there and became a friend of the lovely girl who worked there. Joseph E. Fox and Valley Schiefer were married on February 7, 1907 at Newport, Kentucky. The witnesses were George J. Adams and Elizebetha Seitz. After the wedding Joseph tried working in Newport for the railroad, and later moved to Nashville, Tennessee. Joseph and Valley lived in the Spring Street house with Elizabeth Heiner Fox, his mother.

Several years passed and finally the brothers left the Joseph Street house and started to travel for work. Joseph and Valley moved into the house making it their home. In Edgefield District, two children, Daisey and Florence, were born. Daisey died at ten months and Florence at four years. In 1919, the probate estate of Elizabeth Fox transferred the property, and the Joseph Street and Spring Street houses were sold. Joseph and Valley moved to the country where a new street was built with a few houses in east Nashville away from the town. It was there they bought their first house on Stratford Avenue.

A few years later, Joseph became a house builder for six years. The railroad people formed an association and moved to the location. Joseph Fox built twenty-four houses on Stratford Avenue. In 1922 and 1923 two daughters, Vallie Jo and Charlotte, were born to them. In 1925 a son, Joe Fox, was born. Joseph and Valley worked very hard. She helped on the houses by doing the architectural drawings. They built their dream house. The economic depression of 1929 changed things, business and people's lives. Joseph had to return to the railroad work and he continued to work until 1942.

Joseph and Valley Fox opened the *Nashville Bottle and Barrel Company* at 220 First Avenue, north, two blocks away from brother Bernard's and Charlotte's business. They managed this company from 1936 to 1944. Joseph Fox died on July 24, 1942 in Nashville. The widow, Valley Schiefer Fox, moved to California to be with her daughter, Vallie Jo. There she met and married John Westkamper on August 23, 1945 and resided in Oakland, California. After his death on November 25, 1954, she returned to Nashville, Ten-

Houses Built By
Joseph E. Fox and
his son Joe Fox

nessee to live for ten years near her son, Joseph Fox, Jr.
She died on March 6, 1968 in Washington, D.C. where
her daughter, Charlotte Rita made her home.

Chapter Eight

This story is not in the time of the first migration of people to America, and the early years. It does not, therefore, have to tell of the struggle for a continent against the Indians, along a frontier, with homes built in the wilderness, and even of the planting of colonies, nor of the notions, and the traits of other people.

The descendants of the first people later bring forth a Revolutionary War for independence in 1776, and they were victorious making their declaration of independence from any foreign sovereignty. Thus a new goverment was launched, and new states.

The rights of Americans were inherent with ability and truth. Old America had people who moved westward, and they were great travelers on foot, horseback, light wagons, or river rafts and boats. For years there was a continuous scene of bustle and traveling business. We have the story of how John and Elizabeth were in one scene with these people moving westward.

If John Heiner was an immigrant in the 1830s he would have had Indiana state as a destination after leaving a boat on arrival at an Atlantic seaport. His brothers would have been with him. Two Heiner families lived in Ohio County, Virginia in 1837 when he married. Once Elizabeth married she left the members of her parental family.

It is believed that Elizabeth Heiner later had about fourteen grandchildren but only descendants from Elizabeth Fox.

The daughter, Elizabeth Heiner Fox, had twelve children. Three sons and their wives produced nine children. They were Albert Fox and Mae, Arthur Fox and Mae, Arthur Fox and Emma, and Joseph Fox and Valley. Elizabeth Fox had another grandchild named Richard Bernard Fox. Bernard J. Fox and Charlotte's child was by adoption. Ten grandchildren whose uncles were candy-makers.

Richard Bernard Vaughan Fox was the first grandchild brought home who entered the Fox circle. Richard Fox was born March 22, 1912 in Nashville, Tennessee. Every one of the uncles and aunts were proud of him. The most proud of all was Bernard Joseph Fox, the father, for he put his name up in big letters on the bottle shop as son: B.J. Fox and Son.

Richard Fox married Vivian Peay on October 26, 1935 in Goodletsville, Tennessee. Vivian Peay was born July 30, 1915 in Davidson County, Tennessee. Richard was a farmer on Neely Bend Road in Madison, Tennessee; and manager of B.J. Fox and Son barrel shop in Nashville. Richard and Vivian Fox had five children; Lucy, Judith, Richard, Elaine, and Charles. In 1983 they had thirteen grandchildren and four great grandchildren.[1]

In Tennessee and other places of Ohio, Maryland, and Connecticut, there were five grandchildren born of Elizabeth Fox before 1919. The second Fox born in this generation, and the first of the lineage line, was **Arthur J. Fox,** the son of Arthur and Emma Fox. Arthur Joseph Fox was born on March 13, 1913, in Norwood, Ohio.

Arthur II lived in Cincinnati, Ohio. It was in Cincinnati where the births and marriages of this family and the four daughters took place. Arthur Fox married Martha Uldene Collins on October 24, 1936. Martha was born on December 12, 1913, the daughter of P.B. Collins.

Arthur and Martha Fox owned and worked at the Blue Bird Dining Room in Cincinnati, Ohio, from January 1942 to March 31, 1976. Arthur was the only Fox

ARTHUR FOX II and MARTHA FOX

son to carry on the cooking tradition of the Fox family. Issue: *Barbara, Kathleen, Linda and Carol.*[2]

In 1914, Elizabeth Heiner Fox was to have two granddaughters born, Marie Elizabeth Fox and Daisey Elizabeth Fox. Another granddaughter was born in 1918 and named Florence Elizabeth Fox. In 1917, the first grandson, William Fox was born. These were the years that a World War was taking place in Europe, and the United States were changing. The automobiles were the new transportation, and replaced horse-buggy and horse-wagon. The married Fox sons had really settled down with their families.

Left to Right. Front Row. William Fox, Dorothy Fox Desmond
Back Row. Albert Fox, Marianne Verrell, Marie Fox Verrell

Marie Elizabeth Fox was born on January 21, 1914 in Baltimore, Maryland, the daughter of Albert Henry Fox and Mae Hoyt Fox. They moved to Bridgeport, Connecticut, and there William Fox and Dorothy Fox were born. Marie Fox married Robert Verrell on June 12, 1943, and had children Robert and Marianne. All events took place in Bridgeport, Connecticut. Robert Verrell, the son, was born September 21, 1948; and in adult life is a social worker for the State of Connecticut. Robert remained in single status. Robert Verrell, the father, was born October 14, 1912 in Bridgeport, and died December 11, 1960 in Milford, Connecticut where the family had a home. Robert, Sr. was the son of Kathleen Hefferan Verrell and Peter Verrell.

The daughter, *Marianne Verrell,* was born August

15, 1944 in Bridgeport. She married Thomas Quinn on July 22, 1967 in Milford, Connecticut. They had Megan Elizabeth Quinn who was born November 10, 1978 in Annapolis, Maryland. The Quinn family lives in Arnold, Maryland.

Marie Fox Verrell was a teacher. She married a second time, Bernard McGovern on July 16, 1966 in Milford. He was married to first wife, Margaret Long McGovern who died August 16, 1965. Bernard worked for thirty-two years in credit retail. He was born April 18, 1911 in Boston, Massachusetts.[3]

William Hoyt Fox was born January 22, 1917, the son of Albert and Mae Fox of Connecticut. William was a graduate of Yale University on June 7, 1942. William Fox' military service was in one s. squadron n. Group four, Wing two, Flight Six, Air Force of the United States. In World War II he was at Sheppard Field, Texas, and a First Lieutenant in October 1943. He was a certified public accountant and made his career in New York City.[4]

Dorothy Fox was born April 4, 1924 in Bridgeport. Dorothy Fox married Leo Desmond on June 18, 1949 in Bridgeport, Connecticut. Leo was born there on February 24, 1921, the son of Raymond and Josephine Desmond from Ireland. He has a sister, Jean. Leo was employed by the American Express Card Company. He died on July 3, 1983 in Fairfield, Connecticut, where the family has a home.

Dorothy Fox Desmond was employed as a secretary until 1965. Her son, Brian Desmond was born March 16, 1966. He was a graduate of Notre Dame High in June 1979, and a student at Sacred Heart University at Fairfield, Connecticut.[5]

These men worked in trade business. The grandparents of the Fox heirs lived through the Civil War, and the 1865-1877 reconstruction that took place, organizing labor. With the changes that came, the corporation formed, and owners of the shops entrusted its direction to overseers or managers. All were employed, even children in the factories; ushering in the machine age. In agriculture there were also great changes.

In a few years an Industrial Revolution happened. Working conditions were to worsen, and labor strikes occurred over many years. In August, 1881, at Terre, Indiana, a labor convention was held and planned the American Federation of Labor. Later, a national federation of self-governing trade bodies eventually evolved and formed procedures for keeping order. The 1900 to 1915 years were peaceful and prosperous times.

Daisey Elizabeth Fox was born in 1914, and died at ten months. The family was living at the Springfield Street house with Elizabeth Heiner Fox in Nashville. Around 1916 the family moved into the Joseph Street house for the candy-makers had departed from the house. Florence Elizabeth Fox was born in 1918, and died on March 18, 1921. Her death brought grief to the parents. Daisey and Florence, and Joseph E. Fox, I, later had burials at Cavalry Cemetery in Nashville.

There was no assurance that disease could be avoided, and not much progress in health care, and less in treatment of children's diseases. But there was progress in communication and transportation which unified the country, and helped people. There was the telegraph and lines, and a cable across the Atlantic Ocean, circulating newspapers and magazines, a national postal system delivering letters in a short time, and they were trying to develop the telephone.

The prosperity welcomed the twentieth century but peace was interrupted by an interval of war. The German invasion of Belgium in August, 1914, brought ruin to another country, and World War I broke out. The German submarine warfare torpedoed American merchant vessels and caused a crisis in relations with the United States. Finally, President Woodrow Wilson, who had a theme, "the world must be safe for democracy," asked for a declaration of war in 1917. The hostilities ceased November 11, 1918 with an Armistice.[6] The war gave some political and financial advantage to America. The close of 1919 saw changes and all had not been settled.

In Tennessee there were three more Fox children who were births of Valley Schiefer Fox and Joseph Edward Fox. They had five children; Daisey, Florence, Vallie, Charlotte and Joseph. Only one was to carry the surname of Fox, and the two girls carried later the names of Connors and Whitfield but with these three children born in 1920s there was later to come seventeen grandchildren.

A third daughter was born on March 18, 1922 to Joseph and Valley Fox of Nashville, Tennessee. She was named Valley Joe Fox from her mother's and father's names. Later the spelling of the name was changed to Vallie Jo Fox. She attended catholic schools, college and the University of Tennessee at Knoxville.

Vallie Jo Fox married Robert Edward Whitfield on March 26, 1943 in Nashville. They moved to Contra Costa County, California and settled at Pleasant Hill near Walnut Creek. A chemist job offer brought them to California. Robert and Vallie Jo had four children; Christa, Robert, James David and Joanne.[7] Vallie Jo Whitfield contributed to writing and publishing, real estate and community service.

This daughter is a fourth generation on American soil, and also her first cousins were of the generation. They are the fourth generation descendants of John Heiner and Elizabeth, and the third generation descendants of Joseph George Fox. This is a fraternal line. Since the first immigrants make up the first generation in America, and each child is a measure of another generation; with these families we found a family tree chart with six generations in America. The ancestral origin is mainly from Germany but the marriages bring other ancestral origins from different European countries.

Another daughter, **Charlotte Fanning Fox,** was born June 21, 1923 in Nashville, Tennessee. This daughter of Joseph Edward Fox and Valley Schiefer Fox married first, Carlyle Lewis Stevens, who was born in 1920 in Chattanooga, Tennessee where they married. Issue: *Carolyn Stevens.* Carlyle L. Stevens died at age 24 as a soldier in Germany. He was killed on November 25, 1944 in World War II.

Charlotte Stevens married Joseph Aloysius Connors on September 11, 1945 in San Francisco, California and they moved to his home town of Washington, D.C. and made their home. Her given names were Charlotte Fanning Rita Fox Stevens Connors. Joseph A. Connors was born September 9, 1910 in Washington, D.C. Joseph and Charlotte Rita Connors had seven children: Joseph, Anne, Mary, Claire, Rita, Jane, and a boy, Francis. Joseph Aloysius Connors II, was an attorney and F.B.I. Agent with the Federal Bureau of Investigation. Charlotte Rita Connors contributed to catholic charities and real estate.

A son, Joseph Edward Fox, was born on July 24, 1925. Ollie Mai Tyler was born on February 8, 1925; and both were born in Nashville, Tennessee. Joseph Edward Fox II married Ollie Mai Tyler on December 26, 1942 in Kentucky.

Joseph E. Fox II served in the United States Navy, 1943-1946. He had submarine duty in the Pacific area. Joseph attended the University of California at Berkeley, 1947-1949. He was employed as a box-maker and salesman, 1949-1972, and a post office clerk in 1973 working until retirement.

OLLIE TYLER FOX and JOSEPH E. FOX II

Joseph and Ollie Fox made their home in Madison, Tennessee, in Davidson County. Issue: *Linda, Sandra, Marilyn and Joseph.*[8]

During the opening months of 1920 many curious changes came over America, feeling and style, and work. Noticeable were the inventions of the 1920s which included technicolor, telephoto, radar, sound films, and the basis of the electronic television camera. The mechanical cotton pickers, and the plan for tractors.[9]

In the sky there were airplanes; and in 1919 two Englishmen, Alcock and Brown made a nonstop flight from Newfoundland to Ireland. It was an American pilot, Charles Lindbergh, who alone flew an airplane from New York to Paris across the Atlantic Ocean with the long distance. In May 1927, this outstanding aviation feat attracted widespread attention.

The fashions were different, almost shockingly so in dress. There was the lumberjack or high top boots, short skirts, short heavy jackets, corduroy and new cloths, and newly designed overalls, also new styles of caps, head pieces and hats. It was the roaring twenties.

The temperance societies were many, and the crusade against strong drink had for years been continuous and successful. In 1920, on January the sixteenth, nationwide prohibition went into effect under the Volstead Act. This resulted in the loss of market for several agriculture products which had been planted for liquor.

During these years of prosperity four Fox children were born. Vallie Jo in 1922, Charlotte in 1923, Dorothy in 1924, and Joseph in 1925. There was a growing period and generation of twenty years of time taking place here.

The prosperity of their parents was of short duration. There were new leaders in national offices. It was felt by President Herbert Hoover and his administration that the government should permit big business enterprise to develop without regulation and hindrance. The administration had theories about business and a theory about individualism. It was thought that the progress of the United States had often been due to individualism and these good leaders would lead the way. The unstable monetary methods were allowed to exist and continue when they needed a period of readjustment.

In October 1929, many of the theories were disproved. On Thursday, October 24, 1929, came the stock market crash which started a rapid decline of security values in the stock market in 1929. In 1930-1931 the whole system collapsed into a world-wide financial disaster. The result was a national economic depression in the United States.

In short time, values had shrunken to very low levels. Taxes had risen and the ability to pay had fallen. Government of all kinds had serious curtailment of income, means of exchange of trade froze. All of this

Certificate of Baptism

✝

Church of

St. Michael's

Madison, In. 47250

⟨ This is to Certify ⟩

That __George Fox__

Child of __Joseph Fox__

and __Elizabeth Fox__

born in __Madison, Indiana__
 (CITY)   (STATE)

on the __22nd__ day of __February__ 1 867

was

Baptized

on the __11th__ day of __March__ 1 867

According to the Rite of the Roman Catholic Church

by the Rev. __J. Gillig__

the Sponsors being ⎰ __Henry Hejner__
⎱ __Pathas. Hejner__

as appears from the Baptismal Register of this Church.

Dated __September 12, 1984__

__John L. Fink__
Pastor

103

interrupted industrial enterprise which almost stopped. Farmers found no markets for produce, or for the surplus. The savings of many years in thousands of families were gone. The dark reality was the unemployed citizens. Men waited in bread lines. Women turned attention to food preservation and canning, and became thrifty housewives. The depression years were pitiful years. There were equally great numbers of people toiling in some kind of work for little return.

A new president was elected. Franklin D. Roosevelt promised "a new deal" to the forgotten man — the twelve million unemployed in March 1933. It was Roosevelt's belief that the only thing the people had to fear was fear itself, for it paralyzed needed efforts to convert retreat into advance. With such a spirit in all, they could face common difficulties, for in fact, the concerns were often about material things.[10]

Now two Fox cousins who were born in March 1912 and March 1913 had become adults. Richard B. Fox took a bride in 1935. Arthur J. Fox took a bride in 1936. Richard had two children born in the recovery period of the 1930s. 1937 was the year that Arthur Fox's family began.

To reach this recovery time, the leaders of federal government attempted to bring relief through agencies. They set up the Emergency Relief Centers first. The Works Progress Administration started, and the work program was taken out of the hands of Emergency Relief. The conditions changed.

Arthur J. Fox and Martha Fox of Cincinnati, Ohio, had these children and they grew to adulthood.[11]

Barbara Louise Fox was born on May 27, 1937. She married Harry Joseph Grimes on January 21, 1967. Harry was born on October 7, 1937. No issue. They reside in Nashville, Tennessee. Barbara is a nurse and

Carol & William Victor, Kathleen & John Tenhundfeld, Barbara & Harry Grimes, Linda & Ronald Crawford

Left to Right. FOX SISTERS

professor at Vanderbilt School of Nursing. She entered the school in 1968 and made her career there.

Kathleen Martha Fox was born on March 25, 1939. She married John William Tenhundfeld on October 1, 1966. John was born on May 27, 1930. John Tenhundfeld is an engineer. The family resides in Sharonville, Ohio. John and Kathleen Fox Tenhundfeld's children were born in Cincinnati, Ohio.

1. John William Tenhundfeld, b. September 5, 1967.
2. David Arthur Tenhundfeld, b. September 10, 1968.
3. Paul Henry Tenhundfeld, b. September 10, 1970.
4. Alex James Tenhundfeld, b. April 25, 1972.

Linda Eileen Fox was born on June 19, 1946. Linda Fox married Ronald George Crawford on June 5, 1971. Ronald was born December 6, 1942. The Crawford family resides in Cincinnati, Ohio. Issue.

1. Lisa Ann Crawford, b. July 26, 1976.
2. Sarah Elizabeth Crawford, b. June 17, 1979.
3. Matthew Ronald Crawford, b. June 3, 1984.

Carol Jo Fox was born on May 10, 1948. Carol married William Kelly Victor on September 11, 1971. William was born May 8, 1949. Carol Jo Victor died on June 8, 1972 in Cincinnati, Ohio. No issue.

A family with pretty girls, five sons and three girls make up the fifth generation, and they live in the state of Ohio. Interestingly, the first son, John W. Tenhundfeld was born in 1967 and has become an adult. The last son was born in 1984 and named Matthew Crawford.

Looking back at the 1930s, the country found that the new deal programs were adequate, and they were programs that worked for people who needed them. Congress was busy. The Soil Conservation and Domestic Allotment Act was passed. The Farm Security Administration was created, and the Farm Bureau Agency. The farmer was a man who asked fór help in getting good prices, and the farmer also asked to be allowed to produce without too much tight regulatory restrictions.

There were relocation programs. People were helped to get a location for a better chance. This affected the lives and emotions of people, but it was necessary. The Tennessee Valley Authority helped to build dams for hydroelectric power and regional reconstruction in seven states. Other dams were built where needed and the water was available. Water was the most valuable resource. The Authority helped to produce better health conditions, recreation, agricultural improvement and rural electrification.

The wonder of electricity was even used as a farm security for there were now electric brooders for chicks, electric pumps, preserving kettles, boilers and new equipment, and also more controlled water with dams, which saved the land from erosion and created new liveable land areas.

One Fox farm on Neely Bend Road in Madison, Tennessee, had Richard Fox working the farm. Richard and Vivian Fox had five children, all of them were born in Madison, Tennessee.[12]

Lucy Charlotte Fox was born July 13, 1937. Lucy married Bobby Moore on August 25, 1955 in Madison, Tennessee, and their children were born there.

    1. Terri Moore, b. July 8, 1957. She married David Vick on July 1, 1977.

    2. Kelly Moore, b. February 13, 1964. She married Steve Long on September 1, 1985.

    3. Bryon Moore, boy, b. July 27, 1971.

Judith Fox was born March 7, 1940. She married Jack Barnes on July 7, 1962. This was Jack Barnes' second marriage. He had the care of two children; Joanne Barnes, b. July 14, 1957, and Mary Jacquline Barnes, b. July 9, 1956. Mary Barnes married David Daniel on July 1, 1977.

Judith attended the University of Tennessee. Judith and Jack Barnes had two children: Jeff Barnes, b. December 24, 1964, and Jerry Barnes who was born April 13, 1966.

Richard B. Fox was born September 22, 1947. Richard married Patricia Ann Norman on October 21, 1967. They are the parents of two daughters:

    1. Kimbery A. Fox, b. August 17, 1971

    2. Heather Renay Fox, b. January 21, 1976.

Richard B. Fox II is working the Fox barrel company in Nashville. His father, Richard Fox I, is in retirement.

Elaine Fox was born on October 31, 1952. Elaine married David Adams on December 28, 1973. Issue.

    1. Shelby Lee Adams, b. March 11, 1978.

    2. David Houston Adams, b. December 10, 1980.

Charles Fox born on April 21, 1955. Unmarried. He

FOX FAMILY
Left to Right. Front Row. Richard, Charles, Elaine
Back Row. Judy, Vivian, Richard, Lucy

is an owner of a tool business.

All of Richard and Vivian Fox's children were born in Tennessee, and so were their grandchildren. They stayed together at Madison, Tennessee. They had thirteen grandchildren and four great grandchildren.

The sister of Vivian Peay Fox did the Peay genealogy of her family.

These children of Richard and Vivian have inherited the Fox land and carried on a tradition at Madison, Tennessee.

Chapter Nine

~ ~

From sea to sea this country lay in the middle of one continent, and the land was destined to hold more than Indians. In the early days travel was largely by water and on horseback. The trails of Indians and wild animals became roads after men had forged and traveled the water streams with canoes, rafts, flat boats and schooners.

Shortly before the Revolution of 1776, Daniel Boone blazed a trail through The Cumberland Gap — this gradually became the Wilderness Road of the South. In the north, the national government in 1811 began the construction of a road to the west from Cumberland, Maryland to Wheeling, Virginia reaching there in 1817. This road was an important route to the west during the early period of westward migration. This road was extended and reached its western terminus at Vandalia, Illinois in 1852. The Natchez Road from Nashville to New Orleans, and the Michigan Road from St. Joseph, Michigan to Madison, Indiana, were traveled. Other roads also were developed.

At first, private capital was used for roads, but later the travelers were forced to stop and pay a toll for the use of the road — hence, the name "turnpike". The freight car of the turnpike was the conestoga wagon. In the Far West it was known as "prairie schooner" or the "covered wagon". It did not entirely disappear until the latter part of the nineteenth century. As the country became populated, the importance of transportation increased and a system of highways was developed. In time ox carts, horse-pulled wagons, and stagecoaches went on the highway, and more attention was given to improving roads.

In the north, travel was better in the winter when the ground was frozen and often covered with snow and sleighs could be used.

Railroads

In 1828, the Baltimore and Ohio Railroad laid its first rails. Other railroads followed, with improvements, and in time the country was spanned by a vast network of rails. The United States grew with the acquisition of Oregon in 1846, and California in 1848. The highway from Missouri to California was opened with the rush of people to discover gold in California. Some used the Clipper ships for speed.

A transcontinental railroad was envisioned as linking together the extreme sections of the nation. The Central Pacific Company began at Sacramento and built toward the east; and the Union Pacific began at the east and worked westward. On May 10, 1869, the railroad and long line was completed at Promontory, Utah, north of the Great Salt Lake. The railroad and its network of rails supplanted the stagecoaches.[1]

There was constant experimentation and improvements in vehicles, trains, freight haulers, and boats. Steam power on railroad trains and boats was to give way to engine mechanical power. By 1920 more than 250,000 miles of railroads had been built. This rendered service in passenger transportation and the hauling of freight.

Hence, great things had been accomplished by the people, under God's providence. The effort to control the human future, almost a revolutionary urge to begin a new life for mankind, has been going on for centuries. This human behavior can only bring growth or regres-

WHITFIELD FAMILY
Christa's Wedding 1967
Robert II, Robert I, Christa, Vallie Jo, Joanne, James

sion.

Each human being rises and disappears in the harvest of the ages. Families change, people move, and newness is evident. Anything may happen to any individual or group, or community, for change is inevitable.

The 1940s brought a new rise of human beings in the Fox clan: Judith Fox, 1940; Linda Jo'an Fox 1943; Marianne Verrell 1944; Sandra Fox, 1945; Christa Whitfield, 1945; Linda Fox, 1946; Marilyn Fox, 1947; Richard Fox II, 1947; Robert Verrell, 1948; Carol Fox, 1948; Robert Whitfield II, 1948. The births are mostly girls, consequently, the family lineage takes off into a maternal lineage which has many surnames.

Vallie Jo Fox Whitfield, with her bridegroom, moved in 1943 to Berkeley, California. She had heard

111

the call of the west from the musicians and songsters at Nashville. The railroad train went far to the west, and Joseph Fox I and family had tested the railroad lines, to see how far they went in 1939, when they came to visit the Golden Gate Exhibition.

Vallie Jo Fox married Robert Edward Whitfield on March 26, 1943 in Nashville. They moved to Contra Costa County, California, and settled at Pleasant Hill near Walnut Creek, about thirty miles east of San Francisco, California. A chemist job offer brought them to California. There they found days were extremely beautiful, clear with sunlight, bracing air, and the feeling of belonging sometimes pervaded the mind — a feeling of something to come, vague and undefined, but full of expectation, and interest. This future was to wait. They were in California contributing to the war effort. They settled from 1943 to 1946, and after the war they returned to the east, visiting Tennessee, and living three years in Massachusetts. Robert E. Whitfield attended Harvard University and graduated in 1949 with a Doctor of Philosophy degree in Chemistry. The call of the west was still there; and they did not want to leave mother Fox in California alone. They returned to the Pacific coast, and liked what they saw, and settled down making a home and family. Issue: *Christa, Robert, James David and Joanne.*

Christa Marie Whitfield was born on December 30, 1945 in Berkeley, California. Christa graduated from the University of California at Berkeley, January 1967. She married Roger Lee Bundy on November 18, 1967 in Pleasant Hill, California; and divorced May 1979. Roger L. Bundy was born on April 14, 1941 in San Francisco, California, the son of Robert E. and Gladys Welch Bundy of Antioch. Roger Bundy is a certified public accountant, and attorney in Contra Costa County, California in the city of Antioch.

Roger and Christa Bundy had three children born in Oakland, California.

Jason Edward Bundy, b. July 15, 1970.

Natasha Marie Bundy, b. August 18, 1972.

Justin Alexander Bundy, b. September 6, 1975.

The children attended schools in Walnut Creek, California, where they lived. The mother, Christa Bundy is a teacher. On July 30, 1982, Christa married Charles Wendt Buckingham, who was born August 5, 1947.

Natasha Bundy, Justin Bundy, Jason Bundy, Tara Whitfield

Robert Edward Whitfield, Jr., was born November 21, 1948 in Boston, Massachusetts during the time the father attended Harvard University. Robert known best as Bob, Jr., was a graduate of the University of California at Davis, June 1970. Bob Whitfield wrote the poetry in the book, "LIFE A COLLECTION OF POEMS." [2] Bob, Jr. entered the peace corps, a government program, and was assigned as a teacher to Nalerigu Training College in northern Ghana of West Africa. On October 14, 1971, Robert E. Whitfield was killed by a bolt of lightning in Africa.

James David Whitfield was born in Berkeley,

California on February 21, 1953. On August 30, 1980 he married Tamela Jean Caldwell in Reno, Nevada; and divorced in May 1984. Tamela was born on November 29, 1958 in Oakland, California, the daughter of Floyd and Bonnie Caldwell. To James David Whitfield and Tamela Jean Whitfield, a daughter, Tara Jean Whitfield was born on October 26, 1982 in Walnut Creek, California.

Joanne Vallie Whitfield was born March 14, 1955 in Berkeley, California. She was the fourth child of Robert and Vallie Jo Whitfield. Joanne Whitfield graduated from San Francisco State University, June 14, 1977. Joanne was employed by the San Francisco Printing Company, the Chronicle and Examiner newspapers, 1978-1980. She also is a writer, artist, and editor, and has several publications. Joanne is the contributing editor of Whitfield Books. In 1981, Joanne became an employee of the United States Post Office and became the editor of the post office newsletter. Joanne settled in Sonoma County, California, near the city of Santa Rosa.[3]

The first time the Whitfield parents went to California it was a low populated state, and the country was at war. This World War II began in 1939 when Germany started aggression against their neighbors. England and Russia were opposed. There was a youth movement with the army, and a claim to superiority. The cause of this can be summed up as patriotic vanity, imperialism, and the industrialization of Germany with a planned and prepared arsenal of war materials and strategies. There was a failure in the mental growth and thoughts of generations of Germans. The result was a major war. On December 11, 1941, Germany and Italy declared war against the United States.

On December 7, 1941, Japan attacked the United States navy ships and base at Pearl Harbor in Hawaii.

The Congress of the United States then declared war on Japan. The industry of the United States from 1941 to 1945 had a gigantic effort towards an all-out war. Increases in billets, steel, textiles, grains, and tons of food; millions of gallons of gasoline and oil, machinery, merchandise, automobiles, military ambulances and jeeps, ships, planes, and most hard equipments. There was inflation, strikes, riots, mobilized labor forces, labor wage freeze, wartime regulations, rationing, broken homes, and some loss of freedom.

A global war resulted. Many millions of American men went to battle. Thousands were killed and wounded. On June 6, 1944, D-Day, there was an invasion at France by American men. Eventually over four million allied troops invaded the European area and pushed into Germany.

Men were shoved from island to island in the Pacific Ocean area. No one foresaw the atomic bomb accept the scientists who created it. Our "arsenal of democracy" could not last long since $13 billion had been lend-leased for war materials to our allies.

In 1943, on September the 8th, Italy surrendered. 1945 was a monumental year — the end and the beginning of an era. Germany and Japan collapsed and were forced to accept unconditional surrender to the allied powers. After almost six years of war, Germany, on May 7, 1945 surrendered. Japan surrendered on August 14, 1945.[4]

The end of war brought full restoration of civilian consumer production, collective bargaining, and a return of free markets. It brought a return of men and women to their homelands. William H. Fox, who was in the Air Force, and Joseph E. Fox II, who was in the submarine navy, went home in 1946. Carlyle L. Stevens died in a battle in Germany. Death claimed George Fox, age 77, in 1942, Joseph (Joe) Fox, age 62, in 1942.

Bernard (Ben) Fox, age 66, died on October 28, 1945 at Madison, Tennessee. Albert Fox, age 77, died in 1951. Henrietta (Nettie) Fox, age 82, died in 1954. These deaths were caused mostly by heart and artery diseases. It was an era for the last of the candy-makers — members of a family that did confectionery work from 1855 to 1947.

These Foxes were involved, as all people were, in the post-war years. They accepted, uneasily, all that happened. People found themselves with domestic problems, housing shortages, and inflation. First, there was a food shortage with European people needing twelve million tons of food. The seas were full of a million pounds of edible fish which helped relieve the hunger. Secondly, the housing shortage, and thirdly, inflation, with the living costs rising twenty-nine percent in 1945.

The United States goods and services were valued at $215 billion in 1945, about two-thirds more than in 1939. There were labor disputes. The topics of conversation were rising prices, housing shortage, menace of Russian communism, and atomic energy.

Far from destroying the American arts, there was an impetus in theatres, film and entertainment houses. Older people had broken new trails in music, singing, visual arts, literature, sports, and new medias were developing. American fashion designers urged women to be more relaxed, stressed delicacy and "prettiness."

The American people worked industriously on the domestic scene. The 1950s were a decade of production work in the housing industry and domestic machines. The demand for fast, cheap, prefabricated housing was everywhere. Architects were practical, and designed houses with smaller rooms, and more glass was used in the houses. The builders built on countrysides, low-slung single story homes on smaller lots, and produced the tract house subdivision on acres.

There was mass production of vacuum cleaners, electric ranges, cooking utensils, washing machines and dishwashers. In 1950 the average weekly earnings in industry was up to $60.53, an all time high. In 1953, the population of nearly 161 million enjoyed work and prosperity although a dollar was worth 52¢ compared to the 1935-1939 equivalent.[5]

Producers of newspapers, books, movies, and other forms of communication had an expanding market and new ideas came along each year. In literature, 11,000 titles were published in 1951. Modern arts gained an acceptance. Television had entered the home. It would be a decade later before major television networks were established to provide comprehensive and distinguished coverage of national and international news events on a daily basis.

The Americans had prosperity due to many people's creative talents, research, university output, and opportunity for lucrative investments in the rapidly expanding American industries. The automobile industry was building new cars. The automobile first appeared at the close of the nineteenth century and had gone far in fifty years, a fully developed machine. Great speed had been attained. Highways existed from coast to coast and automobiles now traveled over hard-surfaced roads.

The passenger planes had been flying since 1933 but now they were larger with regular lines and flights, and could travel four hundred miles in an hour. The modern streamline passenger train was on schedule crossing the United States.

— *Signatures* —

Elizabeth Hiner

H. Hiner

Joseph Fox (1832-1888)

Mrs. Elizabeth Fox

Joseph Fox (1884-1942)

J.E. Fox

B.J. Fox

Mrs. Nettie Hager

GEORGE FOX

Chapter Ten

~ ~

In 1945, there was a passenger train crossing the western United States carrying Charlotte Rita Fox Stevens and her two year old daughter, Carolyn Stevens, to Berkeley, California. Charlotte Rita left Tennessee and went to live with her mother. She was settled only a few months when she took a clerk job with the United States Department of Justice, Federal Bureau Of Investigation, in San Francisco. There she met the F.B.I. Agent, Joseph Aloysius Connors II.

Joseph's ancestral lineage was O'Connor of Ireland. His grandfather, **Patrick O'Connor,** was born in County Limerick, Ireland, circa 1839. He came to America. In 1868 or 1869, Patrick O'Connor married Mary Burke at St. Peter's Church, Capitol Hill, Washington, D.C. Patrick O'Connor became Patrick Connors. He was employed as a grave digger at Mt. Olivet Cemetery. About 1887 or 1888, Patrick was working on excavation for a wing of the Capitol building, on the House Office side. A landslide of dirt fell on him, causing his death. He died at Providence Hospital.

Mary Burke Connors, wife of Patrick Connors was born circa 1850 in County Limerick, Ireland. She came to Washington, D.C. when she was twelve years old and attended Notre Dame Academy. Patrick and Mary Connors had seven children: Charles, Michael, Margaret, James, Joseph, Mary (Mamie), and Walter, who was born after his father's death.

The son, **Joseph Aloysius Connors** was born October 26, 1882, in Washington, D.C. He was employed as a railroad fireman and received an appointment to the Metropolitan Police Department where he made his career. Joseph A. Connors married Mary Kate Kenny on November 14, 1906, at St. Dominic's Church, Washington, D.C. They had seven children: Margaret, Kathleen, Joseph A., Jr., Mary, Leo, Albert, and Helen. Joseph A. Connors I died July 7, 1946.

The children grew up in Washington, District Of Columbia, and attended the local schools. Joseph A., Jr. and Kathleen had careers as attorneys. Leo became a policeman. Albert and Margaret entered the Catholic religious life. Mary married and had nine children. Helen married and had three children.

Mary Kate Kenny was born November 26, 1880 in Drimalagh, Castlerea, County Roscommon, Ireland. She came to America around the turn of the century, 1901. Mary first lived in Philadelphia and then moved to Washington, D.C. about 1903. She met Joseph Connors at a Saint Patrick's Day dance. On November 14, 1906, Joseph Connors and Mary Kate Kenny were married at St. Dominic's Church in Washington, D.C.

Mary Kate Connors' parents were Margaret Green, born in County Galway, Ireland, and Patrick Kenny, born in County Roscommon, Ireland.[1]

Mary Kate Connors died May 15, 1965 at Providence Hospital. She and her husband, Joseph, were interred at Mt. Olivet Cemetery.

Her son, **Joseph A. Connors, II** was born in 1910. He spent all of his life except for two years in Washington, D.C., where the members of the Connors families resided. Joseph was transferred on a work assignment to San Francisco, California, and there he met Charlotte Rita Stevens. Joseph Connors and Charlotte Rita Stevens were married on September 11, 1945 in San Francisco. Joseph returned to Washington, D.C. with a family. He adopted Carolyn Connors in 1954. Five daughters and two sons were born in Washington, D.C. Joseph was called Joe Connors. Joe and Rita

120

Connors were parents of eight children. Joseph Aloysius Connors died May 28, 1985 in Washington, D.C.

CONNORS FAMILY

Front Row. Jane, Francis, Claire, Michael McEnrue, Charlotte Rita, Joseph II. *Back Row.* Carolyn, Mary, Anne, Rita, Joseph III

Carolyn Rita Connors was born on October 14, 1942 in Nashville, Tennessee. Carolyn Stevens Connors graduated from Immaculate Junior College in Washington, D.C. in 1962. Raoul J. Benoit and Carolyn Connors were married in December, 1962 in Washington, D.C. and were divorced on March 15, 1984 in Washington, D.C. Raoul was born on May 17, 1931 in New Britain, Connecticut. Raoul's parents are: Dr. Raoul Benoit and Joan Benoit who reside in Clearwater, Florida.

They resided initially in Washington, D.C., then they moved to Montreal in 1966 and then to Frankfurt, Germany in 1970. They purchased a villa in Javea, Spain in 1972 for their summer vacations. They moved back to Washington, D.C. in September, 1973.

Raoul and Carolyn have three daughters.

Michelle Marie Benoit was born on December 27, 1963 in Washington, D.C. Michelle attended college in San Diego, California.

Nicole Aimee Benoit was born on February 17, 1966 in Washington, D.C. Nicole attends college at the University of Denver in Boulder, Colorado.

Wedding Day
Louise and Joseph Connors III

Suzanne Benoit was born on September 17, 1968 in Dollard des Ormeaux, Canada, which is near Montreal. She is a student at the Corcoran School of Art in Washington, D.C.[2]

Joseph Aloysius Connors III was born June 24, 1946 in Washington, D.C. Joseph A. Connors III married Mary Louise Bucklin of Jennings, Louisiana, on June 14, 1969, at Jennings, Louisiana. Joseph A. Connors III is the son of Joseph A. Connors, Jr. and Charlotte Rita Connors of Washington, D.C. and grandson of Joseph A. Connors and Mary Kate Kenny Connors. Mary Louise Connors is the daughter of Herbert George Bucklin and Dora Anna Koll Bucklin who reside at Jennings, Louisiana. Mary Louise was born April 8, 1946 in Jennings, Louisiana.

Joseph graduated from law school at the University of Texas in Austin, Texas, in May, 1973. He received his license to practice in the Texas courts in September, 1973. Louise graduated from the University of Southwestern Louisiana in May, 1968.

Joseph and family settled at McAllen, Texas, in

1974. Then it was a town of 40,000 people. In 1985, the population was approaching 70,000. The Connors family is located ten miles from the Mexican border near the Gulf of Mexico. Joseph A. Connors is a Board Certified Attorney specializing in criminal law. He is a sole practitioner.

Joseph and Louise Connors have two sons: Joseph Aloysius Connors IV, born November 10, 1978 in McAllen, Texas and John Patrick Connors, born November 19, 1982 in McAllen, Texas.[3]

Mary Carmel Connors was born on May 17, 1948 in Washington, D.C. Mary Connors married David Lee Patsel in Washington, D.C. on November 9, 196_. David's parents were Carrie Lee Hodges and Rufus Patsel. David was born on September 10, 1948 in Bethesda, Maryland. David Patsel is employed as a technical engineer with the Columbia Broadcasting System.

Mary owns and operates a construction/remodeling company. She started the company in 1980. Mary and David have four daughters, born in Washington, D.C.

Renee Patsel born on July 8, 1969.
Tara Patsel born on August 25, 1970.
Christina Patsel born on May 14, 1975.
Anna Patsel born on October 5, 1977.

Anne Connors was born on November 16, 1949 in Washington, D.C. She graduated from the Academy of Notre Dame in June, 1968. Anne worked for the U.S. Postal Service from 1968-1978 in Washington, D.C. and West Palm Beach, Florida. Anne joined Strategic Planning Associates in 1979. Strategic Planning Associates is a management consulting firm working with Fortune 500 clients. Anne went to London in November, 1983 to start up the London office. She is the Office Manager.

CONNORS FAMILY
Jane, Anne, Francis, Claire, Mary, Rita, Charlotte Rita

Claire Teresa Connors was born on December 7, 1952 in Washington, D.C. In 1973 she spent one year studying in Aix-en-Provence in France. She graduated from St. Joseph's College in Philadelphia, Pennsylvania in May, 1974. She was employed as a security specialist in the White House Security Office. She graduated from St. Mary's Law School in San Antonio, Texas in June, 1982. She works for the District Attorney's Office in Houston, Texas.

Claire married Michael McEnrue on September 4, 1982 in Washington, D.C. Michael McEnrue was born on November 26, 1947. Michael graduated from Georgetown Law School in 1976. Michael has his own law firm, Mosier, McEnrue & Licata, which was started in 1984 in Houston, Texas.

Rita Marie Connors was born on February 23, 1954 in Washington, D.C. She graduated from St. Patrick's High School in 1973. Rita Connors was employed by the U.S. Postal Service from 1973 to 1986.

Rita married John Berchmans Reardon on January 22, 1983 which was the "social event of the year." John is employed as a police officer for the District of Columbia. John and Rita have two daughters:

Mary Teresa Reardon born on 1/6/84 in Washington, D.C.

Charlotte Anne Reardon born on 10/23/85 in Washington, D.C.

They reside in Bethesda, Maryland.

Jane Francis Connors was born on December 27, 1956 in Washington, D.C. She attended the University of South Carolina and studied nursing. She worked for the mortgage banking firm of York Associates as the Office Manager. Jane started her own company, Columbia Cleaning Services, in October, 1983.

Jane F. Connors married Ken Columbia on April 30, 1983. Kenneth H. Columbia was born on December 26, 1946 in Englewood, New Jersey. He received his B.A. degree from George Washington University in 1977, and his M.B.A. degree in 1980 from George Washington University. Ken started his own company, Columbia Consulting Services, in September, 1985. They reside in Arlington, Virginia.

Francis Russell Connors was born on October 9, 1959. He graduated from the University of South Carolina in May, 1982. Upon graduation he relocated to Houston, Texas and worked for Arthur Andersen & Company. In June, 1985 he moved back to Washington, D.C. and worked for Fannie Mae for one year. He became a certified public accountant in February, 1986. Francis R. Connors works for Enterprise Development Company, a real estate development firm.

On August 23, 1986 in Port Huron, Michigan, Francis Connors married Lauree Anne MacKenzie. Lauree is a graduate of Michigan State University. She graduated in May, 1985. She was employed in the Prince George's County School System as a teacher. Francis is called Frank. Francis and Lauree are residing in Washington, D.C.[4]

All of the Connors were born in Washington, D.C., and the daughters were married there. They all make homes in Washington, D.C. except Jane and Rita Marie. Joseph III and Claire live in Texas. The mother, Charlotte Rita Connors had eleven grandchildren in 1985.[5]

Middle Twentieth Century

The fifth generation of Heiner-Fox descendants gave birth to the sixth generation, who, in 1986, are minors ranging in age from one to twenty years. Each generation of young people experience growth, learning, changes, and the growing-up years until they are eighteen or older.

In the early generations the schools were in session only a few months a year. The home was where children often supplemented their learning. In early generations children learned the mysteries of agriculture, the iron stove, the washboard, and household. Most of all, they learned the English language.

Then educators and districts organized education, required diploma teachers, and attracted more students who stayed longer in schools. After 1900 the primary and secondary educational system was developed. Finally, law required the education of children and their attendance at school. Their education continued for eight, ten, or twelve years. Then the colleges were established and grew and the states established universities for more advanced education.

In 1951, school buildings were designed with sunny congenial expansion of corridors with classrooms on

126

either side. New products for schools made a better environment. Educators sought more classrooms and teachers. In 1956, racial segregation was prohibited in schools. The industrial age had produced much to see and learn about. Every interval of the school age children was crowded with lessons and experiences — the attainment of this humanity, with a sufficient measure of social justice to ensure health, education, and a rough equality of opportunity to most of the children born into the world, would mean such a release and increase of human energy as to open a new phase in human history.

Shortly, by the twenty-first century, 2000 year, the sixth generation older teenagers will be adult and bring forth the seventh generation. These are native born Americans in the United States of the Heiner-Fox lineage. On January 1, 1986, the United States population was 240,468,000 according to the Census Bureau. More people died in the United States in 1985 than in any previous year in the nation's history and more babies were born than in any year since 1965. In 1985, 8.7 out of 1,000 Americans died, lower than the 9.5 rate in 1970. But the number of deaths, steadily increasing since 1982, was a record 2.1 million. Hence, the classical phrase: *"Dust thou art and unto dust thou shalt return. Infinite in Thy vast domain everlasting is God's reign."*

Entrusted to men and women is the earth with all its living species. During the years 1955 to 1985 the industrial age and more is upon the earth.

In 1957, Russia launched the first earth satellite, Sputnik. It opened space technology and astronautics. The all-time United States cumulative death toll in automobile accidents reached 1,265,000 in 1959. Experimentation, research and technology were on the increase.[6]

127

Architects were making changes — that of efficiency builder, since the criterion for a good contract was the speech of construction. New ideas were confined to paper, but these dreams came to physical realities with many industrial laboring people contributing to the creations and the building process.

Thousands of subdivision tract homes were built all across the United States. Architects, builders, trade people also expended their talents on shopping centers, supermarkets, motels, outdoor movies, all in response to a general urbanization and movement away from the central cities. Americans had prosperity. They remodeled the face of their cities with an unprecedented building boom, bought new, bigger, more expensive cars, planned dream homes of greater elegance, flocked in to buy home appliances, gadgets, and color television sets.

Architects contributed to congestion in an area already crowded with traffic and buildings. Roads, access to the buildings, and parking were not completely considered in the redevelopment. Many grand old buildings and their designs and classic edifices fell to the wrecker's ball. Modern architecture took its place with simple graceful design. City planners became permanent staff members of government administration. The elected worked in a political subdivision and the process had human leaders. Highways were turned into freeways to handle the cross-town and through traffic. All the commercial construction brought more traffic congestion and changing commercial situations.

In the period that all of this took place in the city, Joseph Edward Fox was in a suburb of Nashville. In the beginning Joseph G. Fox (1832-1888) had a son, Joseph Edward Fox I (1880-1942), and he had a son, Joseph Edward Fox II (1925—), who had a son, Joseph Edward Fox III (1950—). Two of these men were residents of Nashville, and two men lived near Nashville.

FOX GRANDCHILDREN
Back Row. Lorie Lance, Gary Lance, Ollie Tyler
Fox (grandmother), Joseph Remo, Joseph E. Fox III
Middle Row. Angela Fox, Mary Fox, Jody Fox
Front Row. Casey Jones, Jennifer Remo

Joseph Edward Fox II married Ollie Mai Tyler on December 26, 1942 in Kentucky. Joseph Fox II was born July 24, 1925, and Ollie Mai Tyler was born February 8, 1925. Both were born in Nashville, Tennessee.

Joseph Fox II served in the United States Navy, 1943-1946. He had submarine duty in the Pacific area. Joseph attended the University of California at Berkeley, 1947-1949. He was employed as a box maker and salesman 1949-1972, and a post office clerk in 1973, working until retirement.

Joseph and Ollie Fox made their home in Madison, Tennessee, in Davidson County. He and the others of this name were called Joe Fox. Issue.[7]

Linda Jo Fox, born on November 16, 1943, Nashville, Tennessee. She first married Ronnie Duhl on May 16, 1964, in Madison; and divorced. Linda married her second husband, Walter Remo, April 28, 1969 in Chester, Pennsylvania. Issue.

Walter Remo, b. May 22, 1970.

Michael Remo, b. May 17, 1973.

Jennifer Remo, infant, b. and d. March 1981.

The Remo family made their home in Goodlettsville, Tennessee in 1981.

Sandra Fox was born on November 25, 1945 in Berkeley, California, Alameda County. Sandra first married Gary Lance in Springfield, Tennessee on August 31, 1965; and divorced October 1976. Issue.

Lorie Lance, girl, b. April 19, 1967.

Gary Lance, b. November 25, 1968.

Back Row. Gary Lance, Lorie Lance
Middle Row. Sandra Fox Jones, Hailey Jones
Front Row. Casey Jones

130

Sandra Fox Lance married her second husband Sammy Jones on September 14, 1978. He was a widower with two children: Rodney Jones who was born on November 18, 1965, and Tina Jones, a girl, who was born on November 30, 1967. Sandra and Sammy Jones became parents of Casey Jones, a girl, born on January 14, 1981, and Hailey Jones, a girl, born on December 7, 1984. The four children of Sandra Fox Lance Jones were born in Tennessee. The Jones family with six children reside in Old Hickory, Tennessee. Sammy Jones is a farmer on land next to the Hermitage Historic Site.[8]

Marilyn Fox was born on August 24, 1947, in Berkeley, California. On January 16, 1965 she married Steve Lane in Lafayette, Georgia. Steve is an electrician. Issue.

Dennis Steve Lane, b. July 14, 1966.

Danny Lane, b. January 7, 1970.

Brian Lane, b. October 29, 1974.

The Lane family reside in Nashville, Tennessee.

Joseph Edward Fox III was born January 4, 1950 in Nashville, Tennessee. Joseph Fox III served three years in the United States Army, eighteen months of that time in Vietnam. After his muster-out of the army, he tried farming for a short time. Joseph Fox III is employed as a painting contractor.

Joseph Fox married Mary Lee Smith in Springfield, Tennessee. Mary Lee Smith was born November 23, 1952, in Harlan, Kentucky. Mary Lee Fox works as a licensed practical nurse. Joseph and Mary Lee Fox have four daughters and make their home at Gallatin,

Back Row. Gary Lance, Jr.,
Joseph E. Fox III
Middle Row. Angela Fox
Front Row. Jody Fox, Rachel
Fox, Mary Fox

Mary Smith Fox

Tennessee. Issue.

Jody Ann Fox, b. October 29, 1972 in Nashville, Tennessee.

Angela Fox, b. July 6, 1975 in Franklin, Kentucky.

Mary Elizabeth Fox, b. April 22, 1977 in Gallatin, Tennessee.

Rachel Marie Fox, b. May 10, 1979 in Gallatin, Tennessee.[9]

Twentieth Century Ending

Newspapers and television managed news and suppressed practically nothing. Reports on the Vietnam war lasted five years. The national issues were nuclear power reactors, housing inflation, air pollution, toxic waste, and human issues.

The 1960s had many events which were a little different than those of earlier decades. These events were racial riots, student protests, the black power movement, drugs and narcotics, and increases in crime.

Sixty-four percent of the population were church members. The United States participated in a war in Vietnam. The arsenal of democracy was not successful against Vietnam, and it was a turbulent and hectic time with the drafing of young American men.

In the 1970s the social issues continued and it was a time for change, this time with the women's movement, politics, the "joyless prosperity" of people on welfare, higher divorce rate, and the right of individual choices. In 1974, the scandal of a United States president facing possible impeachment resulted in his resignation.

Building construction peaked in the 1970s and major cities became magnificent metropolitan areas. People settled the issues at the ballot boxes and with their pocketbooks. Public health care was improved. In 1972, the federal deficit rose to $23 billion.[10] The transportation systems had vital links and greatly reduced travel time. These systems made the connections for traveling in the United States. Families tended to be more widely scattered, and depended on transportation. The 1974 business recession was followed by soaring prices to a height not seen before. The economy expansion was hobbled by inflation and recession which were here to stay.[11]

In all of this, Americans have enjoyed the years of peace in the United States. People have taken time for relaxation, recreation, and amusements. Sports, games, and balls of all kinds have interested men and women and kept them occupied. Baseball and football sports have mass spectators. People from trade associations, arts and science, organizations, academies, and businesses have contributed. There are awards, trophies, prizes, and honors. Few can compare with the simple sharing and loving family fun for having a good time.

The Heiner-Fox descendants live in Tennessee, Indiana, Ohio, Connecticut, Maryland, California,

Texas, and Washington, D.C. With this, the others of the surnames, Heiner and Hiner, have not been forgotten. They are included in the book's second edition and continue in chapters ten through fourteen in the hardcover book. There are many biographies and records in the second edition of this book volume and names from several states.

The future and hope for a better world always lays with young people. Census Bureau reported youths' high school diplomas have doubled in mid-1970 since 1950. Important is the quality education and knowledge of the basics. They cannot face the future alone but must do so with other generations and the elders. The 1980s had the good times and more are to come for those who follow the words of the Lord and live in peace and sharing with others. The generation born into the year 2000 has much ahead waiting for them.

Descendants of Joseph G. Fox and Elizabeth Heiner Fox compiled by Vallie Jo Fox Whitfield, 1985.

	Birth Natural		Legal In-laws		
Charlotte Fox Connors	19	and	6	=	25
Dorothy Fox Desmond	6	and	1	=	7
Arthur Fox	11	and	5	=	16
Joseph Fox	20	and	5	=	25
Richard Fox	— 18	and	8	=	26
Marie Fox Verrell McGovern	7	and	4	=	11
Vallie Jo Fox Whitfield	7	and	3	=	11

BLOOD KINSHIPS 70

LEGAL IN-LAWS 50

Children 12
Grandchildren 9
Great grandchildren 25
Great great grandchildren ... 13

Total blood descendents — Fifty-nine Persons.
Total persons, blood, adoptions, in-laws with Fox families — One Hundred Ten Persons.

Heiner Arms

IN HERALDRY, THE DOTS REPRESENT GOLD
ON THE HEINER SHIELD. THE GOLDEN COCK
IN THE LOWER HALF OF THE SHIELD ON A
GREEN SO-CALLED DREIBERG, MEANING
THREE HILLS, IS EXACTLY THE SAME POSI-
TION AS THE THREE BRANCHES OF THE ROSE
IN THE UPPER HALF OF THE SHIELD.

The Heiner Coat of Arms

Signatures

Vallie Jo Whitfield

Vallie Jo Fox

Rita Connors

Charlotte Rita Connors

Joseph E. Fox

Joseph E. Fox

James David Whitfield

James David Whitfield

Anne Connors

Anne Connors

Joanne Whitfield

Joanne Whitfield

Albert H. Fox

Albert H. Fox

ABBREVIATIONS

Ala. .... Alabama
b. .... born
B.A. .... Bachelor of Arts
Bat. .... Battalion
C .... Children
ca. .... circa
Cir. .... Circuit
Co .... Company
d. .... died
D.A.R. .... Daughters of the American Revolution
Dist. .... District
D.C. .... District Clerk
Washington, D.C. .... District of Columbia
Dr. .... Doctor
Exd. .... Extended
F.B.I. .... Federal Bureau of Investigation
HR .... Heiner, Hiner
Ind. .... Indiana
Jos. .... Joseph
Ky. .... Kentucky
M.B.A. .... Masters in Business Administration
Mt. .... Mount
.... Number
No. .... Number
1870s .... 1870 — 1879
p. .... page
P.O. .... Post Office
p.p. .... pages
pri. .... private
RN .... Registered Nurse
s .... South
Sr. .... Senior
ss .... "Subscribed and sworn to"
St .... Saint
St. .... Saint
St .... Street
Sub. .... Subdivision
U.S. .... United States

References and Sources
FIRST EDITION

~~~~~~~~~~~~~~~~~~~~~~~~~~~~~~~~~~~~~~

CHAPTER ONE

1. John Hensell, *"Chronicles Of The Heiner (Hiner) Family 1310-1958"*. (Houston, Texas, Private Print, 1958), Pages 2, 6, 7.
2. *"The Century Dictionary And Cyclopedia"*, (New York, The Century Company, 1906). Maps numbered 85, 86, 87.
3. *"Pennsylvania German Pioneers"*. Volume III, 1785-1808. Volume I, Pages 227, 229. 231.
4. Marcus Lee Hansen, *"The Atlantic Migration 1607-1860"*, (New York, Haysers And Brothers, 1940).
5. Marcus W. Lewis, *"The Development Of Early Emigrant Trails In The United States Of The Mississippi River"*, p. 6. National Genealogical Society, Washington, D.C., No. 3, 1933.

CHAPTER TWO

Heiner — Hiner Family

1. Oral history of Valley Schiefer Fox, 1957.
2. Federal Census 1870, Franklin, Kentucky, Simpson County. Joseph Cox is a mistake, the name should be Joseph Fox. Birthplace for John Hiner is there.
3. Married in a forest and no written record in Ohio County, West Virginia. Proof of marriage in the *"Declaration For Widow's Army Pension,"* May 23, 1865. Circuit Court for Elizabeth Hiner, Jefferson County, Indiana. National Archives record.
4. John Hiner could not be found on Indiana record 1840. Wayne County, Indiana 1840 Census is the only census that has a vital statistic: John Hiner, wife, and one child of their age range in 1840.
5. Old letter from Henry Hiner was written to Elisa. Death certificates of her children, George and "Nettie", give her birthplace as Hosbell, Indiana. May be located south of Madison, Indiana, and north of the boundary line of Clark County, Indiana; and along the Ohio-Kentucky river.
6. Oral history of Joseph E. Fox (1880-1942).

CHAPTER THREE

John Hiner (1811-1864) and Records

1. Arville L. Funk, *"Hoosiers In The Civil War"*, (Chicago, Illinois, Adams Press, 1967), pages 56-63.
2. Civil War and Military Records of John Hiner, and the Pension. National Archives, Washington, D.C.
   References for John (Heiner) Hiner, b. 1811, Germany and d. 1864, Indiana; and Life.

CHAPTER FOUR

John Heiner (1844-1862) and Records

*Footnotes unmarked in the chapter.

1. Civil War military records and the Pension records. National Archives, Washington, D.C.
2. John Heiner military record. Executive Department Indiana, State Commission on Public Records. Archives Division, Indianapolis, Indiana.

CHAPTER FIVE

1. Oral history of Valley Schiefer Fox, 1956.
2. Sisters of Providence Archives, St. Mary of the Woods, Indiana. Application paper of Margaret Heiner, 1872.
3. Marriage record is found in the *"Declaration For Widow's Army Pension,"* May 23, 1865. Circuit Court of Jefferson County, Indiana. National Archives record.
4. Elizabeth Fox's paper with Nettie Fox Hager. Also the death certificate of George Fox.
5. Margaret Heiner, 1872 to 1923. Sisters of Providence Archives, St. Mary of the Woods, Indiana.
6. Mary Heiner Wehrle, 1888 to 1939. Sisters of Providence Archives, St. Mary of the Woods, Indiana.
7. (a) Letter of Fauna Mihalko, Madison, Indiana, September 20, 1984.

> "The old city cemetery is located at the
> foot of the hill where highway number seven
> comes into Madison and St. Joseph is north-

east where highway number sixty-two used to come into town. Until 1950s these were the only two cemeteries in the city, the cemeteries on the hilltop also became city cemeteries."

Deaths and burials were in Madison, Indiana: John Heiner died November 4, 1864. Elizabeth Heiner died July 4, 1901. Henry Hiner died after 1900. Ferdinand Heiner died after 1900. Place of cemeteries is unknown for George Heiner and Atha Heiner. Fauna Mihalko of Madison, Indiana searched for Heiner cemeteries in September 1984. Researcher with the Jefferson County Library.

7. (b) Wards in Madison, Indiana are voting precincts and boundaries change frequently. About the time the Heiner family was living there it was the area east of the courthouse and the sixth ward was in the west side of town. Later they were in second ward in the Business Directory.

8. Hiner appears in Madison Business Directory in 1859, 1867, 1872, 1879.

9. 1860 Federal Census, Madison, Jefferson, Indiana.

10. St. Mary's Church and St. Michael's Church has Baptism, and Confirmation records of Heiner, 1856 to 1870.

CHAPTER SIX

Life of Joseph Fox 1832-1888

1. Naturalization record of Joseph Fox, Jefferson County, Indiana. Circuit Court, T volume, page 92, 1854-1855.

2. No record found verifying the brother's name of Joseph Fox. If two brothers came together to the United States in 1852, the ship passenger list may give the name.

3. Naturalization record of Joseph Fox, Jefferson County, Indiana. Circuit Court, T volume, page 92, 1854-1855.

4. 1860 federal census of Madison, Indiana, Jefferson County.

5. Whitfield, Vallie Jo. *"Whitfield McKeel Fox Schiefer Families."* (Pleasant Hill, California, Whitfield Books, published 1965). Page 414.

This book has the Fox Family Story and genealogy, pages 402 to 438. Mrs. Whitfield apologizes for the mistakes in this first writing of 1965. Fox was never translated from Fuchs. She did not have vital public documents and records then; and relied on the oral history of her mother, cemetery tombstone, and old letters.

Farmers open market was the location where now stands Nashville's courthouse. On this same street across on the north side between First Avenue and Fourth Avenue was the Fox store.

6. 1870 Federal Census, Franklin, Kentucky, Simpson County. Joseph Cox (mistake) on this census is Joseph Fox and his family, dwelling visitation number 117.

7. Whitfield, Vallie Jo. *"Whitfield McKeel Fox Schiefer Families."* (Pleasant Hill, California, Whitfield Books, published 196). Page 414. Oral history of Valley Schiefer. Whitfield published books with print on the Fox family before 1985, and was without the official certificates and documents in County records.

8. Ibid.

9. Greenlawn Cemetery record in the possession of St. Mary's Church, Franklin, Kentucky. Memorandum. Date, Feb. 22, 1873. Name J. Fox. Block A. Lot No. 2, price $25.

10. 1880 Federal Census, Franklin, Simpson County, Kentucky.

11. Oral history of Valley Schiefer Fox, 1956.

12. Death record of Joseph Fox, Tennessee, Davidson County. Roll Number M-2. Book 1874-1889. Page 92. Certificate number 510. Tennessee State Archives, Nashville, Tennessee.

13. The birthdate of Elizabeth Heiner Fox is not clear in records. She chose December 15, 1842, Hawesville, Kentucky as her birthdate, and Kentucky as her place of birth, although she was born in Indiana. We leave it as it was put on her tombstone, which is the same birthdate as appears on the Kentucky federal censuses.

14. The married name of Margaritam Fannie Fox is unknown. She is buried in an old public cemetery in Nashville, Tennessee.

15. These births and death dates of Fox children are from certificates of baptisms, certificates of deaths, federal censuses, cemetery stones, and family descendants.

16. The name was Joseph G. Fox according to two church documents. Misprint in Whitfield Books 1964, 1965 as Joseph J. Fox and Joseph Theodore Fox.

17. Deed Wm. Griffith to Elizabeth Fox, Book 115, page 637. Notebook 10, page 93, 1888 year. Nashville, Tennessee, Davidson County.

18. Deed. Elizabeth Fox. Book 109, page 39. Notebook 9, page 299. Nashville, Tennessee, Davidson County.

19. Will of Elizabeth Fox. Probate January 30, 1919, Minute Book

22, page 121. Will Book 39, page 561. Nashville, Tennessee. Davidson County.

CHAPTER SEVEN

1. Baptisms. St. Michael's Church and St. Mary's Church. Catholic. Madison, Indiana, Jefferson County. Karen Ricketts, Secretary of St. Mary's Church did the search for Heiner-Hiner records in May 1985.
2. Baptisms. St. Mary's Church. Catholic. Franklin, Kentucky, Logan County. Search of records by Mrs. Carlene Suhling, Sacred Heart Church, Russellville, Kentucky, 1985.
3. Joseph Edward Fox accepted another birth date, January 2, 1982 in Nashville, Tennessee. The reason is unknown. Perhaps he never knew the date in Kentucky; he considered himself a native of Nashville, Tennessee.
4. Death Certificate, Nashville, Tennessee, Davidson County. Page 84. Elizabeth Fox.
5. Information submitted by Arthur J. Fox II, 1985.
6. Oral history of Valley Schiefer Fox Westkamper, 1955.
7. Information submitted by Marie Fox Verrell McGovern, July 18, 1985.

CHAPTER EIGHT

1. Richard and Vivian Fox to Vallie Jo Whitfield, August, 1985. Questionnaire Form.
2. Arthur J. Fox to V.J. Whitfield, July 10, 1985. Questionnaire Form.
3. Marie Fox Verrell McGovern to V.J. Whitfield, July 17, 1985. Questionnaire Form.
4. Letter, William Fox to V.J. Whitfield, 1949.
5. Correspondence, Dorothy Desmond, Brian Desmond, Marie McGovern, 1973, 1983, 1985, 1986, 1987.
6. *"The Heritage of America."* Edited by Henry S. Commager and Allan Nevins. (Boston, Mass., Little, Brown and Co., 1951).
7. Vital certificates, Fox and Whitfield records.
8. Correspondences, Charlotte Rita Connors, and Ollie Mai Fox.
9. *"Encyclopedia of American History."* Edited by Richard B. Morris. (New York, N.Y., Harper and Brothers, published 1953), pages 539-540.
10. *"The Heritage of America."* Edited by Henry S. Commager and

Allan Nevins, 1951.
11. Martha Collins Fox to V.J. Whitfield, October, 1983. Letter with births and marriage dates.
12. Richard and Vivian Fox to V.J. Whitfield, August 1985. Questionnaire Form.

CHAPTER NINE

1. Fremont P. Wirth, *"The Development Of America"*, published 1936, pages 539, 544, 553, 555.
2. Bob Whitfield, *"Life A Collection Of Poems"*, (Pleasant Hill, California, Whitfield Books, published 1977).
3. Contributed by Vallie Jo Whitfield, 1986.
4. "The Heritage Of America". Edited by Henry S. Commager and Allan Nevins. (Boston, Mass., Little, Brown and Company, 1951).
5. *"The Encyclopedia Of American Facts And Dates"*, Edited by Gorton Carruth and Associates. (New York, N.Y., Thomas Y. Crowell, publishers, 1979). Seventh edition.

CHAPTER TEN

1. Genealogy of O'Connor to Connors by Kathleen Connors Clements.
2. Connors biographies submitted by Anne Connors to V.J. Whitfield, October, 1986.
3. Biography by Louise Bucklin Connors to V.J. Whitfield, October, 1986.
4. Connors biographies submitted by Anne Connors to V.J. Whitfield, October, 1986.
5. Ibid.
6. *"The Encyclopedia Of American Facts And Dates"*. Edited by Gorton Carruth and Associates. (New York, N.Y., Thomas Y. Crowell, publishers, 1979). Seventh edition.
7. Joseph E. Fox III to V.J. Whitfield, August 6, 1985. Questionnaire Group Form.
8. Conversation via telephone, Sandra Fox Lance Jones to V.J. Whitfield, May 1985.
9. Joseph E. Fox III to V.J. Whitfield, August 6, 1985. Questionnaire Form.
10. *"The Encyclopedia Of American Facts And Dates"*. Edited by Gorton Carruth and Associates, 1979.
11. Ibid.

INDEX

FIRST EDITION

~~~~~~

149

151

153

155